'How much l[...]
to put us bot[...]
ture, Anna?'

'I didn't—'

'Yes, you did.' He reached out, took her by the waist with both hands and pulled her against him with one fluid, magnetic motion.

'You've been doing it quite deliberately. I went along with it because—because I don't rush a woman if she doesn't want to be rushed, but it's more than that, isn't it? What's wrong? *What's wrong?*' he repeated softly and urgently.

'Don't ask me about it, Finn,' she croaked at last. 'Please!'

Weakly, she tilted her face forward and just...sort of...leaned her forehead against his mouth, knowing she was inviting a kiss...a very long kiss...but unable to stop herself...

Lilian Darcy is back in her native Australia with her American historian husband and their four young children. More than ever, writing is a treat for her now, looked forward to and luxuriated in like a hot bath after a hard day. She likes to create modern heroes and heroines with good doses of zest and humour in their make-up, and relishes the opportunity that the medical series gives her for dealing with genuine, gripping drama in romance and in daily life. She finds research fascinating too—everything from attacking learned medical tomes to spending a day in a maternity ward.

Recent titles by the same author:

THE PARAMEDIC'S SECRET

BY
LILIAN DARCY

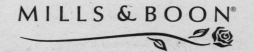

First published in Great Britain 2001
Harlequin Mills & Boon Limited,
Eton House, 18-24 Paradise Road, Richmond, Surrey TW9 1SR

© Lilian Darcy 2001

ISBN 0 263 82675 9

Set in Times Roman 10½ on 12 pt.
03-0701-48172

Printed and bound in Spain
by Litografía Rosés, S.A., Barcelona

CHAPTER ONE

'HERE'S Anna now.'

Escaping the chilly summer rain, Anna Brewster let herself into ambulance headquarters just one minute shy of being late. In the foyer, she was immediately pounced upon by Superintendent Land. There was a man beside him, a stranger, with dark hair and dark eyes, and she was broadsided by a powerful first impression.

Whoever he was, she'd like to draw him. She would use charcoal, and there would be thick lines and dramatic shadings everywhere, especially on his strongly moulded face...

But Superintendent Land was speaking to her. 'Anna, I want to introduce you to our new recruit and your partner for the next two days, Finn McConnell. Finn, this is Anna Brewster.'

Anna's mind suddenly stilled and focused. So this was Finn McConnell. She had been waiting for this moment since a long conversation with her cousin Kendra, just before Christmas. Holding out her hand to join briefly with his in a handshake, she had to fight to hide her reaction to his name. Her reaction to his touch, lingering after their contact had ended, was, no doubt, rooted in the same cause. She didn't want either Vern Land or Finn himself to guess how hostile she was.

'Anna, come with us, will you? I'm going to finish Finn's tour,' Superintendent Land was saying.

She nodded, still struggling to respond appropriately. The reason for her dislike of the man before she'd even

5

met him was personal, not professional, and she wanted to keep the distinction clear.

That's interesting, Finn thought several minutes later. She doesn't like me.

The usual welter of first impressions were coming at him thick and fast. He was scoping out the place, the people, the set-up. Smells and sounds that he knew would soon become so familiar he didn't notice them at all still piqued his senses strongly.

There was the synthetic chemical odour of the recently installed grey carpet in the stand-down rooms, and the metallic rumble of the entry and exit doors to the ambulance bay. It was distinctly different in tone from the sound of the doors at his previous station in Melbourne.

Several hands thrust out to shake his in greeting in the course of the first fifteen minutes, some of them firm, some perfunctory. Formulaic words, nonetheless sincere, overlapped each other.

'Good to meet you, mate.'

'Welcome aboard.'

'Finn, was it?'

'Finn McConnell,' he confirmed.

Faces met his equally formulaic, equally sincere smile with a range of expressions. Sober nods. Casual grins. Distracted frowns. In the background, amongst colleagues who knew each other well, there was a little friendly ribbing.

Somewhere further in the background a phone rang. A microwave pinged. An announcement blared over the loudspeaker. An ambulance tripped the sensor pad in the floor of the garage, opening the exit doors, and nosed its way out. A moment later, its siren began to whoop.

And amidst the confusion of it all, as Vern had introduced him to his working partner for the next two days, flight paramedic Anna Brewster, the strongest impression was this one—*she doesn't like me*.

Finn didn't let it bother him. There was too much else to think about and absorb. In any case, he wasn't in the habit of letting emotions cloud his judgement or throw him off balance, especially when he was, essentially, the one on trial, the one they were all curious about and ready to judge.

'Would you like a coffee first, then we'll get started?' Anna Brewster suggested.

It was a wooden invitation, made perhaps because she felt she had to, or perhaps purely because she craved a coffee herself. Vern had left the two of them to their own devices now. Everyone else had melted away, back to their regular duties.

Finn had known Vern for nine years. For the first six of those years they had worked together in the ambulance service in Melbourne. After Vern's move to Teymouth three years ago to head up the northern division of the Tasmanian Ambulance Service, they'd kept in touch. Last year, Vern had actively head-hunted Finn for this position, telling him, 'I want you, as soon as there's a vacancy here for a flight paramedic. Are you interested?'

Finn had been very interested. Now, seven months later, the promised vacancy had opened up, and here he was.

It was just on eight o'clock, a Monday morning in the middle of January, and the weather was foul outside. You wouldn't have known it was summer. The wind blew in strong, erratic gusts, and chilly grey tufts of cloud tore apart and re-formed as they scudded across the sky. Rain fell in uneven gouts, as if tossed by wild eight year old angels from celestial buckets.

The ambulance garage was freezing. Radiant heaters high on the walls had about as much effect on the temperature as candle flames.

'Coffee would be great,' Finn said, in answer to his partner for the day.

'Vern showed you the staffroom before I arrived, didn't he?' she asked.

'Yes,' he said, then tried some humour. 'The new carpet was a design inspiration. Grey. Tones with the clouds. And I particularly liked the smell.'

She didn't laugh. Just stared at him.

OK, right, well, that's cleared that up, then, he thought. She absolutely doesn't like me. I wonder why...

He crafted a series of plausible reasons and mentally inspected them. Doesn't like men. Doesn't like Scotsmen. Last boyfriend was a Scotsman and ditched her in unpleasant circumstances. Current boyfriend—not a Scotsman—applied for this job and didn't get it. Intuition—which he never trusted in the slightest—said no to all of the above, even the last one, which was the most plausible. Certainly he'd had an easier road into this particular job than a lot of people, but after his experience and the extra qualifications he'd worked hard to obtain in Melbourne he deserved it.

'We have an urn down here as well,' she explained. 'Saves time when all you want is a quick cuppa.'

'Saves the body from the stress of too many extreme temperature fluctuations, too, I suppose. If I remember, the staffroom was warm.'

'Mmm,' she said, and this time she allowed one corner of her mouth to quirk upwards. Couldn't call it a smile. 'We can go upstairs if you want to.'

'Whatever you normally do.'

Anna didn't reply at first, just turned and walked towards one of the storage rooms, which apparently doubled as a tea and coffee station. He followed her, idly noting the neat grace of her walk and the way her dark hair bounced in the middle of her back.

Then she flung back at him over her shoulder, 'If you're complaining about the cold, wait till the next heat wave. The garage is like an oven then.'

'In that case, I'll very much look forward to complaining about that, too,' he said politely.

A small bubble of unwilling laughter escaped from her diaphragm, parting her lips briefly before she clamped them shut again.

Gotcha! Finn thought, starting to enjoy himself.

Maybe she'd recently attended a seminar on gender equality in the workplace and was suffering a temporary bout of militancy. She did look like the type who might not be taken seriously by a certain sort of man. Perhaps she'd suffered from it in the past.

She had a trim figure, just on the petite side of average, neat, high breasts, a tiny, unconscious sashay in her walk. It was somewhat disguised—but not much—by the practical, unisex uniform she wore, consisting of dark blue overalls with yellow bands around the arms and legs.

And her face... Big grey eyes, a soft mouth and fair skin, all framed in dark, voluminous hair that glinted with reddish gold. The prevailing impression, therefore, was of a very attractive woman somewhere in her late twenties, thirty at the outside.

Yes, maybe that was it. She felt she had to prove herself to the new bloke. OK, well, she had nothing to fear from him. He came from a background of strong, heroic women, and was the last man in the world who needed to be told that the right woman could handle anything she wanted to, despite deceptively fragile packaging.

'How do you take it?' she asked.

She had grabbed two ugly floral mugs and spooned in some shiny granules of instant coffee. Now she was tilting the lever on the urn, and boiling water was hissing down.

'Black,' he answered. 'Three sugars.'

Got the reaction he expected.

'That's disgusting!'

'Hits the spot, though.'

'Ugh, no!'

He grinned, took the mug from her grasp and raised his eyebrows in a question which she accurately read.

'Be my guest,' Anna said. 'Mix your own poison.'

'The only way to get it how I want,' he agreed.

She looked around for the sugar to hand to him. From experience, he knew that no one completely believed him about the three sugars. No doubt she would have left each spoon half-empty and forgotten to give it a good stir at the end. While she was still looking, he found an empty jar with a hardened scrape of tired-looking white crystals around the bottom of it.

'Uh…?' Finn held it up.

She rolled her eyes, as if the extra work of refilling the jar for him was the last straw. Then she opened one of the cupboards beneath the bench-top, got out a new packet of sugar and ripped it across the top.

'If you want to wash out the jar…' You can do it yourself was her unstated implication.

Finn shook his head.

She poured, didn't spill a grain. She had wonderful hands, with fine, adept fingers. When she slid the jar across to him, he caught it clumsily then scooped out his three sinful helpings and stirred them in vigorously.

'Are you watching in horrified fascination?' he teased.

'I'm horrified. I wouldn't say fascinated.'

'I guess it betrays my working-class background,' he said.

'Does it?' She sounded very offhand. *Too* offhand. *That's feigned.*

It gave him a jolt. He forgot that he didn't trust intuition, and that he never drew conclusions too soon, and let it all happen like a series of dominoes toppling, until he reached the last one.

She thinks she knows me.

Him, personally? Or his type? It had to be the latter, because they'd never met, either in a professional capacity or a personal one. He'd have remembered. A woman like this. And her name wasn't familiar.

So, yes, Anna had to have condemned him on the strength of type. Not hard, probably. He never attempted to conceal his origins, or the sort of man he was—straightforward, someone who'd come a long way and worked hard for what he had—and most of this could be read in a few sentences of his speech.

'Finn, do you know, your accent *literally* makes me dizzy!' an old girlfriend, a serious student of linguistics and speech, had told him once.

Another old girlfriend—at thirty-three, he'd had a few—used to sigh over it, and tell him he sounded just like her favourite rock singer. Like the former lead singer of a legendary Australian band, Finn had exchanged a working class Glasgow childhood for a working class Australian adolescence, and he had the wandering vowels—spoken in a deep voice with a leathery edge—to prove it.

OK, so how do I handle this? he wondered inwardly. Righteous anger and a deliberate, exponential increase in the tension level between them until they could barely tolerate each other's company?

Ah, life's too short for that!

Simmering and glowering weren't his style. Maybe he was wrong and she had other reasons. Give her the benefit of the doubt. He'd win her over. In his own good time, and hers. And he'd make it fun.

Anna added a generous splash of milk to her coffee then picked it up and led the way out into the large, high-roofed vehicle bay.

'We've got a scheduled transport at nine-thirty,' she said, then broke off and dropped the briskly informative tone. 'How did you get rostered onto a flight crew on your first day, anyhow? No ambulance service I've ever heard of has their new recruits jump in at the deep end, even when they've had a lot of experience elsewhere. And your name wasn't the one on my roster. I was supposed to be working with Steve Quick today and tomorrow.'

She looked indignant and angry, as if his sidestepping of normal procedure was a personal affront and a criminal act. He answered her accusations in order.

'I got rostered on a flight crew because I pointed out to Vern that it made sense, despite being a breach of procedure,' Finn explained. 'Since we've known each other for years and he personally recruited me because of my extra experience in a couple of specific areas, it would have been a waste to send me to the bottom rung for three months, the way new staff usually are. Even so, I wouldn't have won the argument if he hadn't had three of his trained flight paramedics out of action for the next couple of days, and a couple more out of town and hard to reach.'

'Who—?'

'Two are off sick, he didn't tell me their names, and Steve Quick's father died in Brisbane last night. He phoned while I was in Vern's office, so it's not general knowledge yet. He'd be on his way to the airport by now.'

'Oh, poor Steve! I knew his dad had been ill, but...' She bit her lip and blinked a few times.

'Yes, it was bad news,' he agreed. 'So I'm with you instead. And I'm new, as you've pointed out, so fill me in,' he invited. 'As much detail as you like.'

Maybe a willingness to listen, on his part, would soften that steely look around her eyes and mouth.

'OK, then, there's a printout in the office—not the main office, but the one the paramedics use, just off the garage—with the scheduled transports listed, for both road and flight crews. Today we're supposed to take off from the airport at nine-thirty and head out to Redfield to pick up a cardiac patient and fly him to Hobart. Twenty-five minutes flight time to Redfield, thirty-five to Hobart, and twenty back here. Including ground time, turn-out and wrapping up at the end, round trip, door-to-door, will take us about four hours, give or take. After that, we're on call.'

'Here until seven tonight, and at home until seven-thirty in the morning, right?'

'That's right. We're together for the next two days, as you know, then I have four days off, while you work another two with someone else. Fairly standard sort of arrangement. I mean, every service does it a bit differently, I guess. I'll then come back on with a fourth person in the middle of your four days off.'

'I looked at my roster for this month but, of course, it may change now.'

'In any case, it's just sets of names till you get used to it, and get to know everyone,' she agreed. 'It's a bit like one of those old-fashioned English country dances, where you keep changing partners all down the line. Eventually, you get to work with everyone. Sometimes you can go for weeks and hardly set eyes on certain people, if your rosters don't coincide.'

Her tone clearly betrayed the devout hope that this would be the case with the two of them after this initial, unexpected and unwelcome forty-eight hours.

Finn hid a grin behind the orange floral mug and gulped some coffee. Felt the sugar and the caffeine fighting the arctic draughts of the garage as one of the non-urgent patient transport vehicles left the building.

'So if we take off at nine-thirty…' he began.

'Yes, we should leave here by eight-thirty or so, especially on your first day,' she agreed. 'Meanwhile, we'll check our vehicle.'

'Cool!'

Again, she stared at him. *'Cool?'*

He grinned unrepentantly. 'I'm enthusiastic.'

'Apparently.' It was scathing.

Come on; he wanted to tell her. You've got a sense of humour. I know you have. I've already seen a couple of little glimmers. Lighten up. Get over your problem…or at least admit to what it is, because I'm still curious.

He almost warned her straight out, 'You know, I like a challenge.' But his intuition—that thing he didn't trust—told him to play this quietly for the moment, pretend he wasn't aware of her hostility, win her over before he challenged her openly on what she felt and why she felt it.

They drank their coffee as they worked, checking inventory and equipment on the vehicle they would use—car number 121—if called out later in the day as a road ambulance crew. Their stock of morphine had to be checked and signed for, too. There were two road crews already on for the day shift. Anna and Finn would only get called out if a third ambulance was needed, and they'd be limited to call-outs within the city of Teymouth itself, making them easily available for a flight emergency.

During this half-hour of routine, Anna gave no ground and Finn accepted the fact. He rarely wasted his energy on minor battles. If she wanted to behave in this clipped, no-nonsense fashion, he could do so, too.

Then, at exactly eight-thirty, she announced with a dismissive glance at his empty cup, 'Time to go. Better wash that out or the sugar sludge will harden like rock in the bottom.'

'I'm aware of the protocol,' he drawled.

'Are you?' Barbed. She was hinting at something else. Again, he let it go.

She suggested that he take the wheel for their trip to the airport. 'You'll learn the route more quickly that way.'

He agreed.

At least she seemed to be genuinely doing her best to be helpful and informative, rather than carrying her feelings into the professional sphere. He had the impression that she would regard pettiness of that sort as beneath her.

It was a fifteen-minute drive. If you had to, you could, no doubt, do it in ten. On a day like today, with the rain still splashing down, pooling in depressions in the pavement and racing along the gutters, the grey view as they emerged from the Tasmanian Ambulance Service's Teymouth headquarters was not inspiring. Normally, however, it was glorious—all the way down the widening triangle of the Tey valley, past Teymouth's higgledy-piggledy houses and modest CBD, almost to the harbour and the ocean at the river's mouth.

The place wasn't huge—Tasmania's second city after Hobart. But as Hobart was situated on the south-east coast of the roughly triangular island, a very scientific logistical study had shown that Teymouth, two hundred kilometres by road to the north, was the best and most central location for the air ambulance section of the service.

The Beechcraft Kingair B200 aircraft could reach Hobart in twenty minutes of flying time, and Melbourne in just over an hour. Given that certain cases were routinely flown to Melbourne for treatment more specialised or sophisticated than that available at the Royal Hobart Hospital, Teymouth's distance from Melbourne was an important consideration.

Finn had been in the city for just one week, but he'd known before he'd made the move that the pace of Teymouth would suit him far better than Melbourne ever had. Tasmania was gorgeous, a study in contrasts and possibilities, and the lifestyle here actually left room for enjoying all that the place had to offer.

Untamed wilderness and welcoming community, beaches which hosted bathers during hot summer afternoons and penguins at dusk, farms which grew and processed the freshest produce, ranging from sweet ripe raspberries to tangy gourmet cheese.

Finn had rented a little farm cottage, within the required distance limit for both the airport and the T.A.S. headquarters. It was surrounded by a sea of carefully fenced and well-guarded blue-green opium poppies, now past their flowering. They were part of Tasmania's extensive cultivation of the plant for the production of licit opiates, the raw material for legal morphine-based drugs, much of it destined for export. The plants would, no doubt, look spectacular when they were in flower.

Meanwhile, his bedroom looked out on a year-round vista of the Great Western Tiers, hinting at the even wilder country beyond.

Lying in bed last night at ten-thirty, with the curtains open to let the moonlight in, and not in any real hurry for sleep to come, Finn had marvelled at the distances—both physical and metaphorical—he'd covered thus far in his life.

From the slums of Glasgow at thirteen, to this place at thirty-three. From the rude, unquestioning health he'd enjoyed at fifteen to the wreck of a youth that he'd been five years later, his body ravaged by leukaemia and almost more ravaged by the treatments that had eventually cured him. Ironically, he had emerged from the near-fatal illness stronger in both mind and body than his twin brother Craig, who had never known more than a day or two of sickness in his life.

During those late teen years, Finn had had just one goal. To live. Once he'd achieved that, he'd set another in its place. To be strong. He'd taken up martial arts and gained a black belt in tae kwon-do, teaching the discipline for several years both full and part time.

But that hadn't been enough. Growing up in a family that had never valued education, he hadn't finished his schooling. Wouldn't have finished it, he knew, even if his illness hadn't intervened. The years of forced physical inactivity during his illness, however, had taught him the value of education and revealed the quality of his mind. He'd wanted to use it. He hadn't wanted to end up on the industrial scrap heap like his father.

So, at the age of twenty-two, he went back to school, taking adult classes at night to gain his university entrance. He had considered medicine, but knew himself too well to suffer the illusion that he would make a good doctor. He needed something more active, but in that same sphere. Something medical. Something with variety. Something where what he did would *matter* on a life-and-death human level.

And eventually he'd arrived at the work he had just been recruited for—fully qualified flight paramedic for the Tasmanian Ambulance Service, trained in rescue and advanced life support, and now with more than nine years of study, on-the-job training and experience under his belt.

He had enjoyed the work in Melbourne, and expected to enjoy it even more here in Tasmania, where he would travel the length and breadth of the island. He'd waited seven months for this opportunity to come up after Vern's initial approach. Hadn't always waited patiently either, since patience wasn't a notable virtue of his.

Poor, spoiled Kendra! She hadn't quite deserved the grilling he'd given her on the subject of life in Teymouth, and what she knew of medical services there.

'Jeez, Finn! I only did nursing training there for a year before I dropped out!'

'And why *did* you drop out? Weren't you satisfied with—?'

'Nothing like that. The place was fine.' A shrug. Kendra Phillips reacted to many things in life with a shrug. 'I decided teaching aerobics and trying some modelling on the mainland would be more fun. And it is. But, of course, I don't want to do it for ever. If I got married…'

For no good reason, Finn had a nagging sense of guilt about Kendra occasionally. He hadn't seen her for five months, and didn't know where she was or what she was doing these days, though his brother Craig probably did…

'Next left, Finn.' Anna's crisp, impersonal voice cut across thoughts that had strayed way too far in the last few minutes. They were almost at the airport.

'Thanks,' he said.

'Here. Just up ahead.' She yawned hugely.

'Tired?'

'Pete and I got a call-out last night,' she explained. 'Road trauma. Spinal case. Had to pick the patient up in Fryerstown and take him to Melbourne. It was four in the morning by the time we got back, and the outlook for the patient wasn't great.'

She meant she'd been dwelling on it and hadn't slept, even after she'd got to bed. He didn't need her to say it straight out.

'Likely paraplegic,' she went on. 'Turned out I'd been at school with the guy, only he was a few years ahead.'

'Coincidence.'

'Not when it's a call-out to Fryerstown. That's where I'm from, and it's not a huge place. Always sets me on edge when I hear that's where we're picking up from.'

'I'll remember that,' he promised.

'I'm only telling you why I'm tired.'

But there was more to it than that, he could tell. It could have piqued his curiosity if he let it. Once again, he chose not to.

At the airport, she directed him away from the commercial terminal and on a little further to the part where light aircraft were based, and where the aircraft chartered by the ambulance service were hangared. Finn had flown in this type—the Kingair B200—before, so it presented nothing new.

Neither did the pilot. Like Finn, Chris Blackshaw was in his early thirties, young enough to be active, enthusiastic and just a little bit wild in his private life, but old enough to have the required experience. No special training was necessary for a pilot to work in the area of emergency patient transport, just extensive flying hours in a wide range of conditions. The demarcation was clear. The pilot flew the plane, the paramedics dealt with the patients and the medical equipment. Trust in each other's area of competence was paramount.

Today, for example.

'Nice weather for January,' Chris commented.

'Let's not make weather conversation, Chris,' Anna teased. 'Keep your thoughts on wind velocity to yourself, please!'

They grinned at each other, and Finn couldn't help noticing how her voice and manner had lightened. She was really quite beautiful when she smiled. Those grey eyes looked bluer. She lifted her chin and showed white teeth that met in a neat, perfect bite. In the car, she had pulled her hair up into a high ponytail to get it out of the way, and now he could see how long and graceful her neck was, and the clean line of her jaw.

Within half an hour, they were in the air. You couldn't do this work if you were at all squeamish about flying. Although the plane was large enough to require a commercial airstrip, it was far less substantial than most passenger aircraft. In bad weather—like today's—you felt as if you were riding in the stomach of a giant bumblebee, and the roaring drone of the engines only added to this impression.

Flying just above the low clouds, Finn could only conjecture about the vistas he was missing below. There would be rolling farmlands first, then the coastline, dotted with houses that overlooked Bass Strait.

Finally, as they dipped below the clouds again, the wild country of this thinly populated corner of the island appeared below them just before they came in to land at the tiny airport. As far as Finn could see, they appeared to be the only aircraft in operation here at the moment, which didn't surprise him.

Feeling the wind broadsiding the aircraft from the west, he was impressed at Chris's skill in bringing the Kingair smoothly to taxiing speed.

Five minutes after their arrival, the ambulance from Redfield Hospital pulled onto the tarmac. It took just under twenty minutes to effect the hand-over. Oxygen and IV lines had to be checked, as did the ECG leads on the cardiac monitor. A patient required more oxygen in flight than on the ground, and additional medication as well. Brian Charlesworth, aged sixty-four, had already been given drugs for motion sickness and pain, as well as a small dose of tranquilliser for nerves. He also had two stick-on foam pads placed on his chest, one just below the right shoulder and the other against his lower ribs directly beneath the armpit.

'For monitoring,' he was truthfully told, but if necessary—no one ever hoped it would be—two defibrillator paddles could be placed against those same pads to administer a lifesaving jolt of electricity.

After a careful exchange of information and a brief exchange of pleasantries between the two ambulance crews, Mr Charlesworth was loaded aboard via the upward swing of the cargo door. Then the door swung down again and Finn and Anna were left with their patient while Chris spoke to the airport controller, based in Melbourne, in preparation for take-off. At a small airport like this one, the onus was very much on the pilot to back up the distant controller's information with visual checks of his own.

Despite the tranquilliser, Mr Charlesworth was nervous. 'Couldn't pick a calm, sunny day, could I?' he joked feebly.

'Actually, you'll be one of the few people in Tassie who does get to see some sunshine today,' Anna told him easily. Her head looked small and nicely shaped within the confining black arc of the headphones. 'Once we get above the clouds, I mean. It's blue and peaceful up there, as if we're skimming over a sea of cotton wool.'

She had painted a vivid, reassuring picture with those few words, and Brian Charlesworth nodded, seeming a little calmer.

But it didn't last. Chris taxied out to the start of the landing strip, received clearance for take-off from the Melbourne controller and revved up the engines. They screamed, and the plane itself began to judder. The wet black tarmac began to race past, faster and faster, and Finn looked up from checking the ECG tracing once more to find that Mr Charlesworth was gripping Anna's hand hard enough to cut off the circulation, though she wasn't complaining. Sweat beaded near his greying hairline and on his top lip.

OK, so we have a nervous and not particularly stable heart patient, and we're flying into worse weather to the south, Finn thought calmly.

His gaze intersected briefly with Anna's and there was

that little quirk at the corner of her mouth again. He gave a slow blink and a tiny nod in reply. They were going to have trouble with this one.

Their shared awareness of the fact vibrated between them and created a connection that felt disturbing. It was as if someone had taken a big spoon and started stirring up Finn's insides, releasing a cloud of butterflies. Sort of ticklish and frightening. He didn't want to admit to himself that he recognised the source of the feeling. Not yet, anyway.

The trouble with Brian Charlesworth started just five minutes into the flight, as the plane battled and bumped its way through the clouds, making the ride jerky and uncomfortable and necessitating the use of headphones for all of them, including the patient.

The tracing on the cardiac monitor suddenly went flat. Fortunately, both Anna and Finn saw it at once. They checked Mr Charlesworth's pulse, checked the ECG monitor then zapped him with the defibrillator within seconds of it happening. The powerful electrical charge generated a substantial amount of heat and would have burned his skin if it hadn't been for the pads. His chest jerked up from the stretcher then thumped back down and a second later he lifted his head a little and said, frowning, through the headphones, 'What happened?'

'You just had a bit of a faint, Mr Charlesworth,' Anna answered casually.

Her hand rested lightly on his shoulder for a moment, and Finn was too conscious of the grace and warmth of the movement. Conscious, too, of the brief clash of her grey-eyed gaze with his own. Those eyes, fringed with dark lashes, were mesmerising…

Flick. Back they went to Mr Charlesworth again, leaving something nameless behind.

'Oh. Right.' The patient nodded. 'I feel a bit woozy, even though they gave me the medicine. It's rough, isn't it?'

'Just bouncing from cloud to cloud today, I think,' Anna agreed. 'Like a baby's pram going over speed bumps, or something.'

She sounded so relaxed about it that once again Finn had to hide an appreciative smile. She certainly had the right attitude, and a handy set of reassuring images.

Smiles aside, he was still watching the monitor, which was bouncing up and down along with the plane, like everything else.

OK, he registered, the patient's heart's going again, but the rhythm is still unstable.

Anna had seen it, too.

'Something to settle it?' she mouthed. Her shoulder brushed against his and then retreated again.

'Definitely,' he mouthed back, leaning closer.

He couldn't help the movement. It fitted their need to be unobtrusive in their communications with each other, but he noted the way her eyes widened for a tiny moment and the way her lips suddenly parted just enough to admit a swift stream of air before she turned to reach behind her for the new medication.

With no fuss, she added the drug to the swaying IV line and Mr Charlesworth's heart rhythm soon stabilised. He was so busy listening to and feeling every judder and lurch of the plane that he didn't even notice their concern, or the fact that Finn barely took his eye off that monitor for the rest of the thirty-five-minute flight. Anna's hand looked white and pinched from the patient's grip, but she said nothing.

All three of them let out a controlled sigh when the plane finally slowed on the tarmac and the onslaught on their ears and bodies ebbed. Anna removed the patient's headset, grinned rather cheekily at him and said, 'There! Roller-coaster ride over. Welcome back to the ground!'

Here in Hobart, hand-over to a road crew from the Hobart ambulance service took place at the airport. This was accomplished with no fuss or drama today.

Brian Charlesworth seemed relieved to be on the ground and thanked Anna and Finn profusely, although he still didn't know quite how much gratitude he truly owed them. By the time the twenty-minute hand-over was completed, Chris had checked his plane and was waiting for them.

As they waited for clearance for take-off, Finn engineered the conversation quite deliberately, making it as neutral and professional as possible, keeping Anna off her guard but learning quite a lot about her all the same. She took her job seriously, but still managed to smile about it. She didn't panic easily, but she occasionally took things too much to heart.

Now came the twenty minutes of air time between Hobart and Teymouth. Anna had retreated behind her shell of hostility again, after her quietly cheerful professionalism during the Redfield to Hobart flight. She spoke a couple of times to Chris through their headsets but said nothing to Finn. She looked very tired.

By a quarter to one they were back at headquarters and Finn told her, 'It's OK by me if you hide out in the stand-down room for a while.'

'I'm going to grab some lunch first,' she answered. 'Then, yes, I'm going to try and sleep. How about you?'

'Might watch some TV.'

'I meant lunch. Did you bring something?'

'A couple of sandwiches.'

'I'm going to heat some soup in the microwave.

You're welcome to have some.' She used that same cool politeness he was starting to recognise.

'Thanks,' he said. 'But my sandwiches will do. I noticed there's a toaster oven, so I'll toast them and they won't taste like they were made last night.'

'Resourceful,' she commented.

Purely making conversation, Finn realised.

They were alone together in the staffroom as they heated their respective lunches, and it was a little awkward. If she hadn't been giving out such clear vibes to leave her alone, he'd have asked some more questions. Casually personal ones, like what part of Teymouth did she live in and what had she done before her paramedic training.

No one came to it at eighteen, straight out of school. It was actively preferred that new recruits had lived a little first, worked in some other area. The profession drew former teachers, nurses, tradesmen, policemen, and the work and training were both demanding enough that anyone who came to it on impulse didn't stay the course—if they were accepted into it in the first place. Selection procedures were also rigorous, and by the end of it all Tasmanian paramedics were amongst the best trained in Australia.

So where had she been before this? When and why had she left Fryerstown?

Clearly he wasn't going to find out today. He blew out a sigh between his lips. The timer on the toaster oven rattled around to zero and the orange of the heating element inside began to fade. Anna was already eating her soup, spooning it neatly in between mouthfuls of buttered toast while she read the newspaper.

I wonder what she'd do if I just leaned on the table,

took her face between my hands and kissed her? Finn thought.

Suddenly, he understood...or admitted to himself...that he wanted to, and he had to fight a series of too vivid mental images of her response. At face value, she wouldn't like it. She'd push back her chair, leap to her feet. Her eyes would be blazing...not just with anger, though...and her cheeks would be flushed. She'd undoubtedly give him quite a dressing-down.

But beyond that, and beyond every chilly degree of her conduct towards him today, there would be an elemental part of her, he somehow knew, that would respond. The certainty of this understanding glowed inside him like the coals of a fire, dangerous and welcome at the same time.

CHAPTER TWO

'RISE up, sunshine.'

Somewhere on the very edge of Anna's consciousness came the sound of a hand thumping against a door. Flattened palm on wood.

The male voice, newly familiar, came again. 'Rise and shine, Anna. Your pager's not working.'

Groggily, she rolled over and began to swim up out of a sleep that hadn't lasted nearly long enough. She peered at her watch through one eye. Only three-thirty. That meant she'd had a bare hour. Could have done with ten.

'OK, I'm coming in,' said the voice.

'No, it's all right, I'm awake,' she called back, sitting up.

Too late. Finn McConnell had appeared, making her instantly self-conscious about her body, although she'd slept on top of the bed covers in her uniform and therefore wasn't remotely indecent. She wasn't happy with this strange response to the man, but seemed helpless to change it.

'Sorry, but we're called out,' he said.

'I assumed so.' She nodded. 'My pager...'

She unclipped it from her belt and discovered that it had accidentally got switched off, something she'd been too tired to check. Not good. She made a huge effort and shook off the last vestiges of sleep, aware of him in the doorway, watching her.

So aware of him, and of her own body's response to

28

that male bulk. She didn't want to be at all, and perhaps that only made it worse. She knew too much about him, and from the moment when Vern had introduced them this morning, with no explanation about why Steve Quick wasn't working today, she hadn't hidden it well enough. Finn knew something wasn't right.

She was torn between thinking, And so he damn well should, and wishing fervently that she was a whole lot better at hiding her feelings.

Anna wasn't in any hurry for a confrontation. They had to work together for two days, that was all. After this, their rosters might not coincide for weeks, and they'd only connect occasionally.

Her dislike, based purely on what she knew about recent events in Finn's private life, had no bearing on her work or his. Conversely, the fact that her cousin Kendra was, in many ways, a very silly girl had no bearing on the moral issues involved. Finn McConnell had made Kendra pregnant and was so far showing not the remotest sign that he was intending to do the right thing. It wasn't a subject she had time to dwell on just now.

'What are we dealing with?' she asked.

'Priority one. Chest pain.'

'Today's theme.'

'So far. A common one, in our line of work. You drive,' he suggested.

She nodded. 'You can learn the roads when it's not so urgent.'

They reached the vehicle. The keys were dangling in the ignition and she started it smoothly. Seconds later they were out of the garage and on their way, siren singing loudly and lights flashing. A priority one call-out meant they were authorised to use these warning devices, as well as breaking traffic regulations if necessary.

Anna wondered what had taken the first two crews out, so that she and Finn, as back-up, were required. And she wondered what they would find. Chest pain, male patient, age forties, with a question mark. As diagnoses went, it was at the vague end of imprecise. The emergency had been self-reported by the patient, so it could be a case of unwarranted panic. Could even be a hoax. The problem was, you were never sure.

Glancing sideways at Finn for a fraction of a second, meeting only his sober profile, Anna wondered if she could apply those same words to him. Hearsay was inadmissible as evidence in court. With human beings, you could never be sure.

Maybe she was misjudging him. Maybe he was going to take on his share of responsibility for Kendra's unborn child after all. He was here in Teymouth, not on the mainland. Did that mean anything? And Kendra still believed. Or claimed to.

But Kendra was such a bubble-head. She had been spoiled as a child, and hadn't grown up one bit, it often seemed, in the ten years since they'd both left Fryerstown after finishing school. Oh, Lord, it was a mess! And Finn himself had no idea that Anna knew anything about it.

He was an incredibly well put together specimen. Anna didn't have to look at him through Kendra's eyes in order to see the attraction. Tall and solidly built, broad-shouldered, rugged-featured. He wasn't wearing overalls as she was, but had chosen the more formal of the two uniform options today—dark navy blue pants, and a white shirt with navy epaulettes. It suited him.

He wore his dark hair short, as if he didn't care what people thought of the shape of his head, which wasn't perfect and regular and eggy, like a male model, but rather square. His forehead was high and blunt and his jaw stuck out stubbornly, except when he grinned. He had a very wide grin, which crinkled up his dark eyes and made you think of all the wicked but well-intentioned things he must have done as a boy.

He had that weird mish-mash of an accent, which could either be incredibly annoying or incredibly seductive. Probably both.

And Finn was bright. Not the kind of intelligence that had been hot-housed by expensive schooling and conscientious parents, she sensed, but a raw intellect which had flourished like a weed on a garbage heap with no assistance from anyone whatsoever.

He had slipped so smoothly into the job this morning, absorbing each instance of their protocol here being different from that of his former service, and it was impressive enough that he'd talked Vern into letting him do it in the first place. Then he had done everything right with Brian Charlesworth.

Earlier, before they'd set out, he'd even made Anna laugh, although she hadn't wanted to.

Kendra, you picked a good one this time.

They arrived at the address they'd been given, a small, blue, weatherboard cottage with a red-tiled roof, and the sound of the siren died away with a final yelp as Anna switched off the engine.

The place seemed quiet. No one came out to greet them. The front door was closed. Locked, too, they found, after they'd rung the bell and obtained no response.

Finn looked at Anna. 'Force it?'

'Or try round the back. The side gate was open, I noticed. This isn't Melbourne. A lot of people don't lock their back door. Of course it may be a hoax call...'

'Let's do it.'

He led the way, over the roughness of dense, springy couch-grass. Some late sun broke through the thinning clouds, making an untrustworthy promise of fair weather for the morning. They heard a radio playing in the back yard, tuned tinnily to the cricket in some city where it hadn't rained today.

And here was the patient, inert, eyes closed, flung on his back on a low metal and plastic lounging chair, as if in search of the fickle sunshine. He looked to be in his late thirties, rather than the forties this afternoon's ambulance dispatcher had estimated.

'Unconscious...' Anna suggested aloud.

'Asleep,' Finn corrected cheerfully.

And Anna realised immediately that he was right. The man's chest rose and fell, to the accompaniment of a light, fluttering snore. On the cement path beside the lounger stood a small group of beer cans, a mobile phone, the radio, the racing form guide and the remains of some take-away food wrappings. Hamburgers, or fish and chips. The paper was translucent and shiny with grease.

'Eh, mate,' Finn said, reaching down to shake a shoulder. 'Stomach feeling a'right now, then?' His wonky accent sounded stronger and odder. There was something compelling about his voice, which Anna did not want to recognise.

The man opened his eyes blearily. 'Huh?'

'Indigestion gone now?' Finn said.

'Indigestion?'

'You called the ambulance, remember? You were having chest pains.'

'That's right.' Memory returned. 'Hell, they were racking! I'd never had anything like it. *Indigestion?*'

'Can be pretty severe.'

'Never had it in my life.'

'There's a first time for everything. Seriously, though…'

Finn asked some searching questions to confirm what he and Anna were now both pretty sure of. False alarm. As a final check, Anna felt the man's pulse and took an ECG strip. Both were normal, and the man agreed without a blush that he'd overreacted this time.

'Still, you have to take these things seriously,' he said.

And, of course, he was right. It was part of the job. Not nearly as bad as the types who thought the emergency OOO was the appropriate number to phone when they felt like making a prank call or getting a free trip to the hospital for some nice drugs.

Since there was no urgency on the return journey, Finn took the wheel, the siren was silent and Anna gave him a few tips on Teymouth traffic patterns at peak hour—which streets to avoid in which direction, which short cuts worked best. He seemed to absorb it all without fuss as his lean, strong hands manipulated the wheel, and she decided he probably wasn't someone who needed to be told things twice.

Which led to her thinking about a few things she would like to tell him at least twice, which had nothing whatsoever to do with the job. Back at headquarters, she was still thinking about it as she relaxed with a cup of tea in the staffroom. Finn had been sidetracked by today's second ambulance crew, back from the hospital after delivering a woman with acute asthma to the emergency department, and it was a relief to be free of his presence after so many hours together today.

To be honest, she hadn't expected a man like this, despite the over-abundant detail of Kendra's emotional ravings. She had taken most of that with a pinch of salt. As she let the hot, fragrant tea fill her mouth in satisfying gulps, Anna thought back to her last meeting with her cousin.

They had both been in Fryerstown for Christmas. Anna had been rostered on for work the previous Christmas, her first in Teymouth. The Christmas before that she had still been based in Hobart and had made a quick two-day visit home, but Kendra hadn't been there. That meant it had been three years since they had last connected. Still, the old intimacy of their middle teen years had returned straight away, unchanged.

And that was wrong, of course, Anna realised now, pausing with her mug halfway to her lips before she took another thin gulp. Their relationship should have changed in ten years. Why hadn't it?

Her immediate impulse was to blame Kendra herself, but perhaps that was unfair. Yes, it had been Kendra who had grabbed them each a tumbler of down-market, over-sweet cream liqueur on Christmas Eve and pulled Anna into her old bedroom.

Kendra's old bedroom, that was, not Anna's. Anna's room at her parents' house had been converted into 'my craft den' by her mother, and there Mum pottered about making souvenirs for Fryerstown's slowly growing tourist trade. Dabby little paintings on polished cross-cuts of beautiful Tasmanian timber, or picture frames, purchased in bulk and then embellished with pressed flowers, gumnuts, fabric or more painting. To be brutally honest, they weren't all that good. A little twee. But some of them sold and Anna was proud that her mother was resourceful enough to try.

Kendra's mother, Auntie Rona, didn't try anything very much, so she didn't need a 'den' and Kendra's old room was unchanged since she had left it in a blaze of drama and rebellion and wild optimism at eighteen to study nursing in Teymouth.

The room was still painted pink, like a little girl's. It was still crowded with dolls and cuddly toys gathering dust on a set of knick-knack shelves, while the back of the door and most of the wall space was covered in pin-ups of Kendra's teen idols. Jon Bon Jovi, Kevin Costner, several obscure rock stars and some anonymous semi-nude hunks.

But perhaps I'm as guilty as Kendra for going along with it, listening to her, not challenging anything she said, Anna thought now.

Their conversation, as those silly liqueurs had rapidly disappeared, had matched the teenage decor. Only one thing had been different. Kendra had been more than five months pregnant.

But apparently it wasn't a problem.

You see—to tell it in Kendra's way—there were these two brothers she'd met in Melbourne. Twins. Craig and Finn. Both hunks, but Finn was a ten and a half out of ten. They had both worked out at the gym where Kendra taught several aerobics classes each week, despite her lack of formal qualifications in the area.

She had liked Craig at first. Well, he had been the one she'd first met. He was a part-time security guard and bouncer at a nearby nightclub.

But then he'd introduced her to Finn. Sigh. Gorgeous!

Anyway, to cut a long story short—which Kendra *hadn't*—a party, too much to drink. 'Et cetera, et cetera, blah, blah, blah.' Ho hum. In the family way. 'Didn't even think about being careful!' Giggle. These things could happen when you both lost control.

Unfortunate. Kendra had lost her job a short time

later, and she was broke, which was why she was back in Fryerstown, dump though it was, back at her parents', just riding out the pregnancy. Morning sickness, stomach bloating, 'et cetera'. Couldn't teach or model. No choice but Fryerstown. Wasn't going to pressure Finn about a decision on their future.

He was a paramedic, like Anna, 'But at Teymouth.'

'But I'm at Teymouth now!' Anna had exclaimed at that point. 'Didn't Auntie Rona tell you?'

'Oh, probably.' Another wave. 'I guess I didn't take it in.'

'I've been there nearly two years, and there's no one called Finn there.'

'Well, maybe he hasn't started yet. He was waiting for an opening or something. He used to ask me about Teymouth a fair bit at first. I said to him once, ''You're only interested in me 'cos of Teymouth, aren't you, Finn?'' Then I was talking to Craig and he said he'd got the job. Finn had.'

'What's his name.'

'I told you, Finn.'

'Finn what, Kendra?'

A huge yawn and another giggle. 'Sorry, pregnancy makes you so vague. Finn McConnell. You'd know if you'd met him.'

'Of course I would! There's only thirty of us, covering everything from routine patient transport to emergency rescue. Only eight flight paramedics.'

'I mean, you'd *know*, sweetie.' Suggestive drawl. 'He's…'

There followed a lot of rose-coloured detail, which Anna, to be honest, hadn't listened to with her full attention. Kendra hadn't seemed to notice, or care. 'He's got a lot more going for him than Craig. A *lot* more! He's a winner.'

But Anna wasn't interested in that. 'What's he going to do about the baby?' she asked, when she finally got an opportunity to break in. As far as she was concerned, that was always the most important question in a situation like this. Sometimes the only question.

Kendra didn't seem to feel the same way. 'Oh… You know… I don't want to put pressure on him. I think a man's always going to be more interested once it's born. I'm not interested in stuffing up his life, and I'm sure he knows that. I mean, I understand the male perspective, I really do. I think I'm good that way. I think that's why men like me.'

A giggle.

'Well, and certain other attributes of mine. When I get my figure back, and my skin… You see, Anna, I know why men feel trapped, and I just don't want to do that to someone I really care about.'

She probed at this subject for quite a while, drawing on a vocabulary of psycho-babble which Anna privately thought was nonsense. Given a choice, she always preferred to look at life's big issues in a simple way, and as far as she was concerned Kendra's situation *was* simple.

She was single, jobless and pregnant, and the man who was fifty per cent responsible for getting her that way ought to be somehow involved in helping her make the best of the situation. Not that he had to slip a ring on Kendra's finger and declare undying love, if that wasn't how he felt. A baby made very poor glue for sticking two ill-suited people together.

But Finn needed to let Kendra know where she stood, get rid of those rosy fantasies of hers with some plain talking if necessary, and live up to his biological father-hood by making a financial and emotional contribution to the future of his child.

And I'm going to have to bite my tongue to keep from telling him that, Anna realised. Even though it's none of my business.

When her pager buzzed against her hip a few minutes later, she wasn't sorry. Thinking about Kendra, thinking about her cousin's situation and her own past in Fryerstown, it was only making the issues twist more tightly inside her.

As distractions went, however, an urgent call-out to a three-car pile-up in the CBD was effective but not exactly fun.

This time there was no question that she and Finn were wasting their time or their role as back-up to the two main road crews. Wet roads and lapse of driver concentration were the culprits. Two people were seriously injured, and two more needed hospitalisation in Teymouth for minor injuries. One patient was taken directly from the accident scene by helicopter to Royal Hobart with a suspected head injury. Later, once stabilised—if he survived—their own service would probably have to fly him to Melbourne for ongoing treatment in a specialised unit there.

By the time Finn and Anna were back at headquarters, it was time to leave for the day and downgrade to being on call at home.

'Quiet, from the flight perspective,' Finn commented to her. 'About a hundred flights a month from here on average, right?'

'About that,' Anna agreed.

'So we should theoretically run a bit over three a day.'

'"Average" and "theoretically" being the operative words,' she agreed. 'And the day's not over yet.'

Their next call-out came at six-fifteen the next morning, just as Anna had rolled out of bed and was about to lunge for the shower. She shrugged at the disruption to her morning routine. She'd had a shower last night as she always did as soon as she arrived home from work. Sometimes the job wasn't very clean. But the service aimed at a turn-out time of one hour outside normal working hours, and that did not include the luxury of a shower.

And this one was definitely going to be serious. A thirty-eight-year-old female patient, admitted to Fryerstown Hospital in unstoppable and rapidly progressing premature labor with triplets at just twenty-six weeks gestation. Two aircraft would be needed. Anna and Finn would each fly in separate planes to Hobart to pick up a neonatal transfer pack and a NETS team, consisting of a neonatal specialist and a neonatal intensive care nurse.

The teams would be flown to Fryerstown, where they would spend several hours stabilising each baby for transport to Melbourne Children's Hospital and handing over to the neonatal staff there. The two Hobart teams would then be returned to Hobart before the planes could finally head for home base in Teymouth once more. The five legs of the journey and ground time in between would take the whole day and much of the night.

Finn had just arrived at the ambulance service's airport office when Anna pulled into the parking area. She hadn't asked him yesterday where he lived. She'd told herself she hadn't wanted to know that much about his circumstances. Maybe he already had another woman in tow, after leaving Kendra in the lurch.

But today she was more curious, or perhaps simply less stubborn about admitting it. Either he lived closer to the airport than she did, or he was lightning fast at getting out the door, because Anna knew she hadn't wasted any time.

They had swapped uniforms. He was wearing overalls, and she had on the more formal outfit.

'I grabbed it off the hangers automatically. Why?' she muttered to herself.

Because it's Fryerstown, she realised.

It hadn't struck her before, but there were other times when she'd been called out from home for a trip to Fryerstown, and each time she'd chosen the dark pants and crisp white shirt with its natty epaulettes.

To show everyone in my home town how far I've come in life? Or to show myself?

Finn looked as good in the overalls as he had in the shirt and trousers. Looked even better when still rumpled from sleep than he had when fresh and neatly groomed as he had been yesterday. He hadn't had time to shave, and his new growth of beard was pushing through as thick and fast as a tropical forest. One side of the open collar on his overalls was folded in, and Anna had to resist a strong urge to reach up and tidy it for him. Her fingers tingled suddenly, and she closed them into a fist.

She said instead, 'Lucky you got a good workout with the equipment yesterday. You'll be all right on your own?'

'I'll spend the time between here and Hobart running through it to make absolutely sure,' he said, acknowledging her right to ask this question with a brief nod.

'But so far there's been nothing significantly different from what we had and how we used it in Melbourne.'

'You go with Chris, then,' Anna said, and again he nodded, this time so quickly that she knew he'd already planned to suggest this himself. 'I'll go with Rick.'

Both pilots were already there, turning over their engines and running through their pre-flight checks. In the office, the phone rang and it was a message from Fryerstown Hospital. The first baby had already been born, by Caesarean. She was in better shape than she might have been, and she was surviving so far. The hospital had the equipment but not the experienced specialists, so it had to be a matter of prayer and teeth-gritting determination.

The second baby, born just ten minutes ago, hadn't made it, and they hoped he would turn out to be the smallest of the three. His placenta had been smaller than the first little girl's, and all the Fryerstown staff's attempts at resuscitation hadn't enabled him to breathe or keep his little heart going.

Finn's comment was practical, and Anna herself had been around long enough not to find it callous. 'Solves one problem,' he said laconically. 'I wasn't sure we'd get a plane off the ground with two babies, two teams and two neo-transport units.'

The units weighed a good hundred kilograms each, containing a portable incubator, oxygen, compressed air and monitoring equipment.

'This way,' he went on, 'at least each baby gets its own plane.'

The aircraft were both ready. Anna and Finn closed the office again and separated. They'd meet up in transit in Hobart, no doubt in a flurry of early morning activity as the teams and the equipment came aboard.

There would be separate flights, spaced a few minutes apart, to Fryerstown, and then a painful hiatus once each specialist team had been delivered to the hospital. Stabilising a tiny premature baby for transport could take several hours.

By the time they reached Hobart at five to eight, the Hobart teams were waiting at the airport with their transport cots, which needed special brackets to anchor them in the plane. The teams had already received a report on the birth of the third baby—a boy, bigger and stronger than the little one who'd died, not as big as the girl but doing well.

Picturing tiny Fryerstown Hospital with its outdated collection of brick and fibro buildings, Anna knew how tough it must be for all concerned. And she was thankful, at heart, that her role between Fryerstown and Melbourne would be limited to dealing with flight safety issues, assisting the NETS team with the equipment and responding to their needs and instructions. Today, hers wasn't the ultimate life-or-death responsibility.

She gave a standard pre-flight safety briefing to the NETS team, pointing out emergency exits and explaining the use of life jackets in case of a water landing, as much of their flying time today would take place over the waters of Bass Strait. When this was done, she had time to wonder about the parents of the babies. They were a tourist couple. The end of the second trimester seemed like an odd time to chose for a holiday in Tasmania's rugged south-west when you were pregnant with triplets.

Neonatologist Paul Swanson made the same comment during the flight from Hobart, through clear weather and over increasingly rugged and sparsely populated terrain. He had received more detailed information from both

Fryerstown and the patient's own obstetrics specialist in Melbourne by this time, and so far he didn't seem impressed.

'These women!' he complained loudly into his headset. 'They get to thirty-five and suddenly their career isn't enough and they want a new lifestyle accessory. Doesn't happen within a week, so they go and badger a fertility specialist. Treatment is premature and over-enthusiastic, and three embryos implant.

'Well, great. They wanted it all, and now they're getting it all. Only they won't accept that it's going to change their lives in any way whatsoever. This one went against Gordon Leggett's express advice in taking this holiday and, boom, this happens.' He shook his head. 'It's her own fault, and it makes me angry.'

'But, Paul,' the neonatal intensive care nurse said sensibly and carefully, 'wouldn't it be all the worse for the mother now—for both parents—to feel that it's their fault? And couldn't this have happened to her at home? You know it could!'

He snorted, then admitted, 'I'm just mouthing off, Sarah. Want to get my hands on those babies before someone does something ghastly. She was having pains for two hours before she did anything about it, apparently. The safest way to transport premmie babies is *in utero*. This aircraft could probably have got her to Melbourne for delivery if she'd made a move sooner, and none of this would be happening.'

'Only a few more minutes,' Nurse Sarah Comstock said, as sensibly as before.

Anna recognised now, too, that this was Paul Swanson's way of expressing and partially relieving the same tension that they all felt.

The plane touched down in Fryerstown at ten past nine.

CHAPTER THREE

HOME.

It was jarring for Anna, as always, to find herself suddenly here, at a few hours' notice. It felt like Lewis Carroll's looking-glass land, not quite the same Fryerstown that she knew so well—the place where she had been born, at the same hospital as the three premmie babies, and had spent her first eighteen years. This was a sort of parallel universe Fryerstown, which she moved through in a bubble, separate from everyone else.

Normally, whether a flight was a routine patient transport or a medical emergency, she wasn't here for long. It could take less than an hour for patient hand-over and equipment checks. Sometimes she didn't even leave the airport, and only saw the town itself before landing and after take off, passing the windows of the plane at some crazy, tilted angle so that it took her some seconds to recognise landmarks. That's the mine manager's house. Those are the slag heaps and the waste water channels. There's Sulphur Street.

Today was different. Her first task, and Finn's, was to assist with the transfer of the equipment from the two planes to the ambulances, driven today by local volunteer crews. Once this was done, and each ambulance had left for the hospital with the two neonatal teams on board, the urgency ceased.

Anna and Rick made another check of the plane's equipment, Rick from a pilot's perspective and Anna from a medical one. Had anything been damaged or

moved or disconnected during flight? Knowing the rep-
ertoire of likely drugs and supplies for the trip to
Melbourne, were they all to hand and in order?

Parked adjacent to them, Chris and Finn were doing
the same thing in the second aircraft. Finn took a little
longer at the task than Anna did, and she knew he was
taking extra care that everything was right. This wasn't
a scenario he'd have wanted to plunge into on his second
day in a job where he'd had to argue to bypass the usual
gradual augmentation of responsibility.

Sorry you were so pushy now? she could have asked.
She thought about it, then rejected the idea. He might
not catch the humour.

In any case, so far there had been no suggestion whatsoever that he wasn't equipped to handle anything that
was thrown at him.

He came over to her when they were both finished,
grinned easily at her and said, 'So, this is your native
soil, right?'

'If you want to put it that way.'

'Is there somewhere in this town where we can get
something to eat?'

At which point it fully hit home.

That's right. I'm here for the next few hours with
nothing to do, and it looks as if Finn McConnell is expecting me to play host.

She glanced around for the pilots, and crossed Rick
off the list at once. He was a quiet man, trying to turn
his thirty years of experience as a pilot into a blockbuster
adventure novel. If ever he had a spare moment, he'd be
holed up in some flimsy shack of an airport office with
his laptop, his Thermos and the packed meals his wife
always prepared for him, rattling away on the keyboard,

slurping coffee and munching. He wouldn't be interested in driving into town.

Chris was making plans of his own. 'It's possible,' he said, 'that I have a girlfriend in this town.'

A quick phone call apparently confirmed that he did, and he wore a wide grin when he informed Anna and Finn, 'She's picking me up in ten minutes. Nice. Haven't seen her in a year.'

'Would she be open to giving us a lift into town?' Finn asked, as if he and Anna were joined at the hip.

She drew in a breath to protest, then thought better of it. Not really fair to abandon the man, and it wasn't as if there was any lure in the prospect of spending what might be some hours in Fryerstown on her own.

Mum and Dad were away on their annual January trip to a caravan at a beach camping ground on the east coast. Her brother Rod lived down in Strahan, operating a tourist boat. She'd lost contact years ago with any friends from school who'd stayed in Fryerstown.

You could see Kendra.

Ugh. They'd had a fight just after Christmas. Was Anna wrong in thinking Kendra had promoted it quite energetically?

'You're *always* critical of my choices!' she had claimed. 'You *always* make it clear that you would have done better in my situation! You have no respect for me! You never have! You look down on me! Well, you can just get down off your high horse, you smug, snooty-nosed…!' As Kendra herself would have said, Et cetera.

Anna was still waiting for an apology. Eventually, she suspected, she would be the one to mend fences without one. Underneath, she was very fond of her spoiled, way-ward cousin, and perhaps there was some truth in some of Kendra's accusations, too.

At the moment, however, Kendra's ex-lover seemed like the lesser of two evils.

Unless she took the bull by the horns for the baby's sake and played matchmaker, got Chris's obliging part-time girlfriend to drop both herself and Finn off at Auntie Rona's little green fibro house in Oxide Street for a rapturous reconciliation.

Oh, brilliant idea! She wanted to stay out of the situation, not place herself strategically as a punching bag between the two of them.

Chris's Maddy had a 'the more the merrier' response to the prospect of two more passengers in her ancient and tiny European car, which meant that Finn and Anna were squashed into the back seat.

So squashed, in fact, once Chris had slid the front passenger seat back as far as it would go, that Finn had to turn his legs sideways and stretch his big arm across the back of the rear seat. Anna had the choice of scrunching herself up hard against the window handle and looking like a scared rabbit, or letting her limbs fall more naturally and having them nudge against Finn's thigh and torso. She went with the latter option.

Regretted it.

Fryerstown airport was some minutes from the town itself. With the rugged nature of the surrounding terrain, a closer location had not been possible. The road into town was sealed and smooth, but it wound sickeningly from side to side and up and down. With each change of direction, their bodies lurched together, goading him to mutter at one point, 'I'm not doing this on purpose, you know.'

'I know,' she muttered back fiercely. 'Neither am I.'

'Got that straight, then.' Suddenly he grinned. 'You know what? I'm not going to fight it any more.'

For a few seconds she didn't know what he meant, then his right arm dropped onto her shoulder, he shimmied himself a few inches closer and now, instead of colliding, they moved in unison on the bends and the pressure between them was steady and warm.

Her skin crawled and heat began to pool inside her. Oh, this was just great! Her body responded to his with a life of its own. She felt the softness of her breast nudge against his side, and knew he was aware of it, too. He seemed relaxed, totally confident in the rightness of their contact, not pushing it but not fighting it either.

Something was very wrong with the springs of the seat. This car was beyond old, barely fit to be on the road. Their shared weight was making the seat sink in the middle, pushing them even more heavily against each other. Effectively, she was nestled right into his arm.

Arms.

There was nowhere for that big left limb to go except across the front of his body and onto her thigh or hip. Her choice. The hip felt too intimate, sending a jet of heat straight for the core of her, just inches away, but when she used an elbow to nudge his hand lower, its flattened weight on her trouser-clad thigh felt even worse.

Well, even *better*, actually, but in this case better *was* worse!

Oh, it was crazy!

He gave a lazy growl of laughter at the way she kept trying to wriggle into a safer position. 'Hope you don't get car sick!'

'That's not the problem!'

In front, Chris and Maddy were catching up on their news with a fervency which suggested they'd last seen each other drifting in opposite directions in separate life-boats shortly after a shipwreck. Maddy was gabbling out her life story, Chris kept interjecting 'No! You're joking!' and Maddy wasn't paying the requisite attention to the road.

Screech! She took a bend too fast, and Anna felt Finn's face...his lips and nose...against her hair. It tickled, and was almost like a kiss.

'Mmm! Honey and almond,' he murmured, before another bend changed their weight distribution again.

'Peach and almond,' Anna corrected, as if it mattered. The man was a connoisseur of shampoos? That sounded dangerous.

Speaking of danger...

'Hey,' he said to the front seat, with a mix of cajoling and desperation, 'Maddy, we're ambulance drivers. It really hurts us to have you driving like this. Can you, please, develop a greater interest in the road?'

'I'll tell you later, Chris,' Maddy said obediently, and they reached the approach to town in one piece. 'Where am I taking you?' Maddy wanted to know.

'Drop us opposite Cassidy's—that would be fine,' Anna said.

'They tore down Cassidy's two years ago.'

'OK, opposite the big slab of old concrete floor where Cassidy's used to be.'

Maddy wasn't a Fryerstown native, clearly. If she had been, she would still have said 'Cassidy's', although the old-fashioned department store no longer existed, and 'the mine manager's house', although it was now an expensive bed-and-breakfast, and 'the railhead', although the rails themselves were now rusted to pieces and grass grew up through the metalled bed of the track. Copper was still mined in Fryerstown, on a small scale, but it went out by truck these days.

'Here we are,' Maddy said. 'Do I have to pick you up again?'

'No,' Finn answered. 'We'll be staying in touch with the hospital, and the ambulances will take us back to the airport when they're ready.' Chris would be paged, too, of course.

'Right.' Maddy didn't seem concerned about the emergency which had brought them to Fryerstown, fortunately. Anna didn't feel like talking about it right now. The team would be at the hospital by this time, working over the two tiny babies…if both of them still lived.

Their temperatures and blood gases needed to be stabilised, their respiration and fluids brought up to the right levels. Were they breathing on their own? They'd need IV lines for fluids and nutrients to keep up their strength. More than one IV, probably. One to a vein in the scalp, perhaps. A central line to the chest. Not desirable, but often necessary. They would be stuck with sensors and taped with wires and tubes until there was hardly a square inch of skin left free. Their little nappies would be the size of folded sandwich bags, and almost as thin, and their urinary output would be measured to the millilitre.

Meanwhile…

Chris and Maddy drove off, after Maddy had barely brought the car to a halt for Anna and Finn to get out. It was fairly obvious that the two of them were going to rush off to Maddy's and leap into bed. Whether any form of future commitment was on the agenda, Anna didn't care to speculate.

Meanwhile… Meanwhile…

The sun was shining on the slab of concrete that used

to be Cassidy's. The miners' monument and fountain ran with bubbling water. The surrounding mountains dreamed in the summer air, bare of trees and clad only in stark spills of rock in colours of rust red, yellow ochre, dirty pink, bark brown and leathery white. The streets, with their mean little fibro or weatherboard dwellings and brave shopfronts were quiet.

Lord, but it was an ugly town!

No! No, it wasn't, it was *beautiful*. It *was*! The colours of those mountains were so rich. The skies were so hugely blue when it was fine, and so dramatically clouded or silkily fogged when it wasn't.

The green little gardens that people had made were like oases, not on streets like shadeless Oxide Street, which marched straight up the hill and boasted only tired yellow lawns, but on the two streets that bordered innocent, unpolluted Dangar's Creek, tucked just below the mine manager's house high on a hill.

And, not so far away, there was the lushness of the temperate rainforests on the way down to Strahan and the dark waters of Macquarie Harbour.

How was it possible to hate and love this town the way Anna did? To love all those rich earth colours on the mountains, even though she knew they were the result of stripping the ancient forests until not a tree was left to stem the ravages of erosion, and of poisoning the air with chemicals from the copper smelter. To hate the lack of choices for its young people, even though in so many ways she loved the uncompromising isolation of the place. To hate the poisonous dominance of the mine, even though she loved the stories of the early days, when copper ore had first been found here, and hard lives had been lived by the miners who'd wrested the mineral from the earth.

'Anna...?' Finn was watching her carefully.

Lord, how long had she been standing like that, staring up at the mountains and breathing the morning air?

'I'm sorry,' she said automatically.

'What for?'

'You're probably starving,' she improvised.

'Aren't you?'

'Yes, actually,' she admitted.

'Then let's eat. There must be somewhere.'

'We'll head up the main street. There are a couple of cafés. You choose.'

'If you like.'

The choice came down to the Wild Rivers Café, which doubled as a gallery, selling local paintings and hand-crafted Tasmanian wood products, and the Paradise Take Away, which would serve you a deliciously greasy breakfast until eleven, and then metamorphose into a pizza place, serving deliciously greasy pizzas, until ten at night.

Finn picked the Paradise, and she was a little surprised. The atmosphere at Wild Rivers was far more genteel.

Somehow he didn't need her to ask him about it, and explained when she hadn't even spoken, 'My theory is that the servings will be bigger at this one.'

She laughed. 'They will be.'

Anna was starting to relax a little more, Finn decided. Earlier it hadn't been hard to sense her strong, conflicting moods. In the background, there was the grey wash of tension they all felt about the two fragile lives which were the reason for this whole exercise. Overlying that, for Anna, was a complex pattern of feeling about her memories of this place and her past here.

He could easily see how someone could get attuned

to the raw beauty of the town, how its poisonous chemistry could seep deep into their bones.

Then, in the car...Oh, boy, the car. He hadn't known whether to fight it or go along with it. He certainly hadn't wanted to give her the impression that he was using the car's movement as an excuse for touching her, but in the end there hadn't been a choice. The cramped space, the wrecked seat springs, Maddy's wild driving. He couldn't have kept himself from touching her if he'd tried. And, of course, he hadn't tried, because he hadn't wanted to.

She had felt so good. She had *smelt* so good. He'd almost named the scents in her shampoo correctly. And if his masculine perception was worth anything at all, she had been every bit as aware of him as he had been of her. It hadn't been one-sided.

At the moment, sitting opposite her at a table in the corner and watching her study the menu, he felt as if they were the only people in the whole world who mattered, and as if this interlude in Fryerstown might never come to an end.

They both ordered a big, hot breakfast of eggs, bacon, sausages, grilled tomatoes and toast, washed down with orange juice and coffee. She winced at his dollops of sugar again. There were three other people there, just finishing off their own late breakfasts, but otherwise the place was deserted. Outside, even the main street was quiet.

'Isn't this the tourist season?' Finn asked.

'For what it's worth,' she agreed. 'A lot of people prefer Strahan. It's by the ocean. There's fishing, and the Gordon River cruises. But Fryerstown is starting to invest in tourism now. It's a good jumping-off point for some of the wilderness hiking routes.'

'Would you like to see it develop in that direction?'

'If it keeps the town alive, gives people employment, of course I would.'

'I thought you might be happy to see the place die a natural death once the mine finally closes altogether. I get the impression not all your memories are happy ones.'

'That's not— Well, yes,' she revised. 'It *is* true. It was hard, growing up here at a time when the mine was scaling down its operations year by year. There was a sense that you had to leave or go under, yet most of us knew our parents couldn't afford to finance an education elsewhere.'

'What did you do?'

'I went to Hobart and half killed myself, working my way through art school, then realised at the end of it that, not being as talented as I'd once thought, all I'd qualified myself for was a very minor career as a commercial artist, and it wasn't what I wanted at all.'

'So you became an ambulance officer.'

'So I became an ambulance officer,' she agreed. 'I still draw a fair bit in my spare time, but professionally I realised I wanted to do something that mattered. I did the full paramedic training, moved to Teymouth, did the flight training—and here I am.'

'Here you are.' He decided to take the statement literally, though he knew she hadn't meant it that way. 'No one you want to go and see while we're here?'

'My parents are away.' That was all she said, and he could tell that she was holding something back, and that it was an effort for her.

He thought about pushing, then decided against it. Her body language was pretty explicit. She'd sat up higher in her chair, pushed back a little. The confiding posture, which had suggested she might be willing to reveal more, was gone, and her expression was cool.

'What would you like to do next?' Anna enquired politely. 'We'll probably still have another hour or more after this, even if things are going well.'

'Go for a walk?' he suggested. 'End up at the hospital? I'd like to see the babies, if possible, to see what we're in for while we're still not under any pressure. Get to know everyone a bit. I expect I'll be involved in flying the parents up to Melbourne in a day or two.'

'Yes, I suppose you will,' Anna agreed. 'I'll be off but, yes, the mother ought to be fit enough to travel by tomorrow or Thursday, when you're on with…'

'Simon Petty, I think,' Finn supplied.

'He's good. You'll like him.'

'I like you.'

It just slipped out. What was that old line? 'Caution, do not engage mouth before putting brain into gear.' Well, he'd just done it. It had definitely not been the right time to slip in a line like that, although the more time he spent with her, the more he meant it.

'Fast worker, aren't you?' was her sour comment.

Exactly why he shouldn't have spoken. Despite those fierce moments of awareness in Maddy's car, and the soft shreds of her past self, her inner self, which Anna had begun to reveal to him—like strips of bright, torn silk, he thought fancifully—she hadn't abandoned her hostility. Not one bit. She had only…forgotten about it at times, because of the strength of the elemental connection between them.

Which was interesting. Mysterious. Why should there be that conflict inside her? Almost as if she didn't want to be hostile but for some reason felt she had to.

'Fast worker. That's a loaded term,' he told her.

'You're right.'

'You prefer it the old-fashioned way?'

'I prefer a man to at least try to pretend that there's more than one thing on his mind.'

'Even when it's on your mind just as much?'

Snap! Up went her head. Her jaw dropped half an inch and then froze tight. The muscles around her eyes tightened, and one hand came to clutch at the top of her very professional white shirt, where just one button at the neck was unfastened. Time seemed to slow and he waited, had room to think, during her few crucial seconds of silence, What's she going to say? Is she going to deny it?

No.

'I can't help that,' she blurted.

'But you would if you could?'

'Yes!'

'As a general rule, or purely in relation to me?'

'As a general rule,' she parroted deliberately, 'I don't have this problem with my co-workers.'

'I'm flattered.'

'And I—I guess you should be,' she admitted confusedly.

Anna Brewster, this flushed, was a pretty amazing sight. How could you describe that soft pink blooming on her cheeks? What had happened to her eyes? They had been plain blue-grey. Now they were like rainy pools, reflecting dark storm clouds. Breath was coming in and out over a bottom lip that was suddenly moist because she'd licked it nervously, and she was wiping a hand up through her hair in a vain attempt to mask her face. Finn had a vivid image of those slender fingers raking across the top of his own head.

'And I should…apologise,' she went on. 'I'm sorry, I—'

'Why? Why should you apologise?' Finn demanded. Surely she wasn't scared of her response to him, was she?

No, he realised. No, it wasn't that.

She had gathered her inner resources now. 'Because it's wrong, and it's going to go away as soon as I can make it. Believe that, Finn!'

'Should I?' He spoke his thoughts aloud. 'On the one hand, you're a strong-willed woman. On the other, what we were both feeling in the car was pretty strong, too.'

'It wasn't.' He couldn't believe Anna was denying it like that, and just listen to her reasoning! 'It was purely to do with the steamy atmosphere being generated in the front seat,' she said. 'With those two talking each other's clothes off and Maddy driving as if she'd forget how to do it—and I don't mean how to drive—if she didn't get home in the next three minutes…'

He laughed. Her voice had risen without her being aware of it, and the waitress, who had just arrived to take their plates away and offer more coffee, had pricked up her ears.

'Yes, all right, it's funny,' Anna said.

'And it's not true. What was happening to us had nothing to do with what was happening in the front seat. But if that's your story, if that's the best you can come up with, I'm not going to push it.'

'No. Good.' She gave a short nod, her colour still high.

Aagh! This was maddening! Now she almost looked disappointed, as if a part of her had wanted him to keep at her about it. It was too confusing. The only course of action seemed to be to retire from the fray. Temporarily, of course.

If Anna thought that he was the kind of man to be put off by the wishy-washy protests she'd given him so far, then she was very much mistaken. Sure, if he'd been in any doubt whatsoever about their chemistry, but the fact that she'd admitted it herself, bathed in all that graceful confusion...

Finn's groin tightened, and so did his determination. No, this was very definitely not finished yet.

'I'll pay,' Anna said abruptly.

They had both waved away the waitress's suggestion of more coffee a minute ago. Finn threw a crumpled ten dollar note onto the table and Anna squashed it in her hand and went up to the cash resister at the counter. He watched her, appreciative of the way the dark navy fabric of her uniform trousers spread so smoothly and firmly across her neatly rounded backside.

She was chatting to the waitress and he tuned in to the conversation.

'Yes, I'm in Teymouth now. I'm a flight paramedic. We're on a call-out, just here for an hour or two, waiting for two patients to be stabilised.'

They finished with a couple of pleasantries, then she came back to the table and handed him some loose change. 'Here.'

'Thanks.' A quick tally told him that she had scrupulously split their bill, and it seemed easier just to pocket the money than to argue the point. If it was a point of honour with her, he respected that.

'She was in my brother's year at school. I didn't recognise her until she said something,' Anna was saying. 'She's lost weight.'

'Sorry?'

'The waitress.'

'Oh, right,' he said, then added, 'Still up for that walk?'

She nodded, so he stood up and they left the café together.

It was a form of claustrophobia, Anna decided as they began to walk back down the main street. In an open space, with physical exercise to occupy her body, she wouldn't feel the same awareness of him. The secret link between them in the car had been brought out into the open at the Paradise Café, and it was crazy of her to be disappointed because he hadn't pushed just a little further.

She almost wanted to confront him with it. Yes, I'm attracted to you, but if you think I'm going to fall into bed with the man who made Kendra pregnant...

It would have been so satisfying to say it, to set those tiny dark hairs on the back of his neck standing on end with shock, because clearly he had no idea that she knew anything about it. If he had, he would surely have said something.

She was starting to wonder if he'd even bothered to remember...or find out...that Kendra was here in Fryerstown. He hadn't mentioned her by name, or even hinted that he knew anyone in this town.

I'll tell him...

But Anna didn't want to stoop to that. Create a scene? Sordid, and hitting a little too close to home. Mainlanders sometimes joked about the inbreeding of rural Tasmanians. It wasn't fair or accurate, but there had been a couple of families she knew here and in other nearby towns whose shifting relationships were like something out of a sleazy court case. Her own life could so easily have ended up that way as well.

This was one of the things Anna had wanted to escape when she'd left Fryerstown at eighteen. She'd been dizzily in love with Russell Hoxton that year, and certain that their future would be a shared one. The pregnancy scare had taught her otherwise. Russell had been so horrified when she'd told him of her suspicions. And then, in the end, she hadn't been pregnant at all.

Or so she had assumed ignorantly back then when her period arrived at last, four weeks late and unusually heavy and painful. Now she understood that she'd probably had a miscarriage, and that was an odd, unpleasant feeling. To know belatedly that there had once been a baby, and she should have grieved. Should she grieve now, years later?

Impossible, really. Russell, once full of such grand plans for leaving Fryerstown and conquering the world, still lived here, working at the local petrol station. At twenty, even before Anna had left for Hobart, he'd fathered a daughter with Lisa Berg. Less than a year after that he'd fathered another one with Vanessa Simmonds.

I could be like Lisa and Vanessa, she knew. We'd have gone to play-group together, with our three children, half-siblings and almost the same age. Or we'd have fought like angry cats over Russell, who wouldn't really have cared about any of us.

That's not what I want.

She hadn't wanted such a tangle of tenuous connections and dishonoured commitments then with Russell, and she didn't want one now with Finn. She shuddered.

Finn was oblivious. He took a deep, appreciative breath and grinned at her. 'The air's fresh.'

'It is today,' she answered. 'It isn't always. It never used to be.'

The grin turned crooked, more complicated. 'For the

moment,' he said softly, 'I'm only interested in today. Tell me about that big house on the hill.'

They crossed Malachite Street and took a short cut over the derelict concrete floor of Cassidy's, talking as they went. Just a few hundred metres away was the Lyell River, still hopelessly poisoned from the ore processing, and a thick, bright rust orange in colour. It was like a running wound through the town, and didn't begin to get clearer until miles further downstream, where gradually nature somehow miraculously managed to filter out the worst of it before it tumbled, still undrinkable, into Macquarie Harbour.

'It's terrible,' Finn said, studying the water from the car and pedestrian bridge that crossed over it.

'Like it's running paint, not water,' she agreed. 'When I was a child, I used to think that rivers and creeks had personalities... No, I shouldn't be telling this story yet. Wait and see.'

She led the way across the bridge and up into the half-hidden houses behind the grand eminence dominated by the mine manager's house. It was cooler and shadier here. Some people had restored the cheap old houses prettily, and tall tree ferns grew in many places.

Out of the mountains behind the town and down between the houses came tumbling clear Dangar's Creek, and Anna and Finn stood on a much smaller bridge and watched as it scurried on downstream to its confluence with the Lyell River fifty metres further on.

Anna took up her story again. 'I used to feel so sorry for Dangar's Creek,' she said. 'Once, my brother and I tried to dam it up and divert its course. We got as far as flooding someone's garden, then Dad showed us a map and convinced us that Dangar's immolation in the poisoned Lyell was one of life's more inevitable calamities.

There's simply nowhere else for the poor little creek to go.

'He couldn't understand why we cared. He couldn't see that for us Dangar's was alive, like a happy, misbehaving little hobgoblin, while the Lyell was garishly dead, and the moment where the clear water met and mingled with that orange paint was just *painful* to us.'

Finn was silent for a moment. 'You're amazing, Anna,' he finally said.

'Why? Because it can still make me cry?' She brushed away a tear with her knuckle and forced a little laugh. 'That's not amazing, that's just silly.'

'Because you can still invest a mountain creek with personality,' he said seriously. 'Because of what you feel about this town. It *is* amazing. What's your brother doing these days?'

'Rod? He's living in Strahan, piloting a tour boat up the Gordon River.'

'Where the water is pure?'

'Where the water is pure,' she agreed.

They grinned crookedly at each other, and she was alarmed at how much those grins communicated, back and forth.

'And your mother?' he asked. 'What does she get up to?'

'She makes souvenirs.'

'And your dad?'

'Watches sport, drinks beer and collects his pension. I love him, but we don't have a lot to say to each other. He's from the school of thought that believes parenting is a woman's responsibility so, you know, the connections were just never made.'

'Like my father, too, all of that.'

'Really?' Anna nodded, not entirely surprised.

'Something in common.'

'Maybe they watch different sports.'

'Maybe they do,' he agreed, humouring her. But he was right. It *was* something in common, and not the only thing by any means…

Hell, I want to kiss her! Finn thought. Hold her, touch her. 'Kiss' isn't right. *Drink* her. Take her. Give myself to her. It's… It's…

Something he would have to harbour inside himself until the timing was right, which it most definitely wasn't yet. She had folded her arms across her body. That fluent, betraying body language of hers once again. Don't touch! it said. I might want it, but don't do it, all the same.

A'right, Anna, he thought, I'll respect all that confusing conflict inside you, but I'm not going to let you forget what your body is telling you.

They were still standing on the little bridge, leaning rather uncomfortably on the splintery wooden railing. Deliberately, he eased a little closer in order to get a better view of the steps that zigzagged up towards the big house on the hill. His movement had the side benefit of bringing him almost close enough to brush her arm with his, and he knew she had noticed.

She moved a tiny bit away, but not as far as she could have moved if she'd really wanted to. Not nearly as far. The realisation ignited an incandescent spark of promise in Finn's future, and he smiled down at Dangar's Creek as if the water were an old friend.

CHAPTER FOUR

'THERE'S a stick insect on your shoulder. Stop a minute, Anna.'

'Oh!'

'Scared of them?'

'Not really, but—'

'Hold still. It's quite small.'

Obediently, Anna stood on the path. Finn lifted her collar out of the way with one hand, moving very slowly and carefully. She felt the back of his hand brush her jaw. He stuck out the index finger of his other hand and began to coax the brownish-green creature onto it. It took a few moments.

'Hold *very* still,' he said.

He had his gaze fixed on the insect, and Anna couldn't help watching his eyes. They were as dark as a gypsy's and so full and honestly expressive of everything that he was made of—intelligence, humour, warmth, curiosity…And kindness.

Most men would just have flicked the insect off into the bushes and thought no more about it, but Finn didn't. Instead, he let it stalk awkwardly around his hand as it explored. He hadn't stepped away from Anna, so they were still standing very close, both intent on the creature now.

'Want to hold him?' Finn said.

'Um…'

'Go on.'

He didn't wait for her to agree, just took her hand

gently and positioned it next to his other wrist. The stick insect had begun to march up his arm. The dark hairs that curled there caught at its legs like long grass. Anna could feel the hairs, too.

Finn had gorgeous forearms, below the rolled blue sleeves of his overalls—smooth, hair-ruffled skin covering solid, ropey muscles and square, strong wrists.

'Come on, Fred,' he said, nudging the creature with his finger. It wouldn't go in the right direction. 'Press your arm along mine,' he told Anna, and she did so.

His head was bent in concentration, and she felt his forehead brush her hair. The possibility of a kiss was palpable in the air between them, and she kept expecting him to initiate it—her breathing was getting shallower and shallower—but he didn't, and finally the insect stepped across to her arm and began its confused sentry duty up and down.

She gave a tiny screech. It tickled, and felt dry and clingy. Creepy! The kind of sensation it would take a while to get used to.

'What do you think?' Finn still hadn't moved.

'It does look incredibly like a stick. But the poor thing is going to need trauma counselling soon if we don't put it back where it belongs.'

'Want to do it?'

'OK.'

They found a tree leaning over the low fence at the front of someone's garden, and she rested her arm on a branch and waited for Fred to make a rapid and rapturous return to his habitat, but he didn't.

'Not very bright, is he?' she said.

'Here…' Finn's touch again, this time from just one finger sliding along the skin of her arm till the insect clung and he could put it off onto a branch. She watched every hair on her arm stand up to attention and felt her nerve-endings there buzz with life. 'I guess that's the end of nature study for today.' He looked at his watch. 'We should get to the hospital. It's getting on for twelve. They should be ready soon.'

'I feel out of touch,' she said.

'They'd have paged us if they needed us.'

'I know, but…'

Anna couldn't admit to how distracted she'd been over the past couple of hours. She was wearing the uniform, but that was about it. If he guessed that she kept wondering why it was that he hadn't kissed her…

They walked along Conglomerate Street, crossed the poisoned river by a bridge further down and then headed up Calcite Street to the hospital on the other side of the narrow river valley.

'I love the street names in this place,' Finn commented drily.

'It's a company town,' Anna said. 'Some bright spark in mine management in the 1930s thought it would be cute to name them all after rocks and minerals and refining processes. As if mining wasn't dominant enough here already.'

'I take it you'd rather we were strolling up Primrose Lane, or something.'

'Well, it isn't great fun to grow up in Sulphur Street. But, no, not Primrose. Why not name them after some of the pioneering miners, though? Or the explorers?'

'I take your point. You're proud of this town's human heritage, rather than its past generation of mineral wealth.'

'Something like that. I'm sorry, you don't need to get embroiled in the complexity of my feelings about Fryerstown. Here's the hospital.'

He didn't answer, but she felt the brief brush of his fingers against her palm, once more sending a prickling warmth all the way up her arm. For a moment, she thought he was going to hold her hand, but then he'd stopped to let her pass through the entry door ahead of him.

Another mind-bending and too abrupt journey through the looking-glass. That was how it felt. There were only a few other patients at the hospital at the moment, all minor cases. No one was waiting in Casualty. But the sense of urgency in the air was huge.

'They were about to page you,' said the middle-aged receptionist at the front desk, not someone Anna knew.

'Ready to go?' Finn asked.

'Not yet. Likely to be another half an hour, apparently.'

'Problems?'

'Of course! But go on through and hear it from the experts.'

The atmosphere in the hospital's very basic paediatric unit was hectic and tense. Dr Swanson was keeping no one in any doubt about his feelings. The parents of the babies were in the recovery annexe next to the operating theatre where the babies had been delivered, and were fortunately well out of earshot. The mother was showing no signs of any post-partum complication, which was one blessing.

The boy and girl both had names now, written in black felt-tip on cards at the foot of each transport unit. The boy, who would be going with Anna and her team, was Matthew Thomas, and the girl was Ashley Kate. They didn't seem quite human enough to have names, so red and thin and fragile, with skin that was almost translucent as the fat layer beneath it had not yet formed.

Neither Finn nor Anna distracted anyone with questions, just absorbed what they needed to know by listening and looking. As expected, Matthew seemed to be
having a harder time. His oxygen saturation level was
lower, and the rate on his respirator was consequently
higher. As Anna watched, Dr Swanson was cursing under his breath, trying to put another IV line into veins
that would be like fine threads. It was distressing the
baby, but it couldn't be helped, and when the specialist
achieved success at last his relief was very evident.

Finn's team was almost ready to depart, but when they
did so, in a flurry of activity five minutes later, Anna
hardly noticed, too absorbed in what was happening to
Matthew.

'I still don't like his oxygen sat. We've got to get it
up, but those lungs are so fragile,' Dr Swanson was saying. 'I'm going to turn up the rate. Just a fraction. And
we're going to wait.'

They did, for another hour, by which time Anna assumed Finn and his plane would be long gone. But when
little Matthew's blood oxygen levels, heart rate and temperature were finally satisfactory and they drove back
out to the airport, she found the plane still there, and
both Rick and Chris going over mechanical checks while
the medical team inside balanced on a knife-edge of tension. Should they wait this out? Try and fly in another
plane? Take the baby back to the hospital?

'What's the problem?' she asked Finn, who was
prowling back and forth between pilots and neonatal
team, clearly wishing there was more he could do.

'Some damned warning light keeps going on when it
shouldn't be going on. Or at least, if it should be going
on, it means there's a problem and we can't take off.
But Chris thinks it's the light that's at fault, not the en-

gine thing, only they have to check to make sure, because if it *is* the engine we'll drop out of the sky. And you probably didn't understand half of that but, sorry, I'm not a pilot, I'm a paramedic, and—'

'Feeling totally useless either way.' Anna nodded. 'Finn, we have to head out.' She was getting signals from her team, and Rick had returned to his aircraft to complete his own pre-flight checks.

Fortunately, nothing was amiss, and they achieved a quick, fluid departure. Anna hooked up the transport unit's oxygen equipment to the plane's supply, and plugged in the power as well, to save the battery for use in transit. She discussed cabin pressure and temperature with Dr Swanson, and communicated his requirements to Rick in the pilot's seat.

After take-off, she reported the flight's status back to the service's control centre. During all of this, Matthew's condition remained satisfactory, despite the stress of movement and noise.

Once safely in the air, Rick was able to report, via the headphones, 'OK, Chris has clearance for take-off now, too. It was just the light.'

'Thank heaven for small mercies!' Dr Swanson muttered, then said to Anna impatiently, 'There's a rattle between the unit and the frame-thing. This thing here. Can you fix that? Pad it with something? We just don't need any more noise and vibration, and it's driving me mad.'

Having expected to share Finn's recent sense of helplessness, Anna found herself busy for the rest of the flight. Dr Swanson was demanding. The cabin wasn't warm enough after all. Could she find a better position for the IV fluid bag? How many minutes out of Melbourne were they, and how was the vehicle, which was already waiting for them at the terminal, set up? Those brackets would need changing again, wouldn't they?

She dealt with everything as efficiently and clearly as she could, and was rewarded, on landing at Melbourne's Essendon Airport in the late afternoon, with a brief, 'Good work, everyone. He's hanging in there.'

Then came the bustle of another transfer. Unhooking the oxygen and power, locking the unit into the brackets in the ambulance, reporting to the Victorian service's drivers, who would navigate tangled Melbourne traffic while Anna remained in the back of the vehicle with the NETS team, dealing with the equipment.

Finn's plane was coming in to land just as her own crew left the terminal, but they caught up to each other as the transfer at Melbourne Children's was completed in the early evening. Scribbled case notes had to be handed over, and a vital oral report on each baby's condition given by the NETS staff to the hospital's neonatal specialists.

Finally, both teams could let go of their tension. The babies had survived the transfer without any apparent worsening of their status, and for Finn and Anna this was the best that could be hoped for. Since the babies' parents lived in Melbourne, there would be no return flight to Tasmania, and news of the ultimate outcome for these two tiny infants would probably never reach them.

'Which is a mixed blessing,' Finn commented to Anna, as they stood waiting for the two NETS teams to wind up their hand-over. Both having filled the same role in all of this, they were natural allies, and she didn't question the fact that they were standing together, a little apart from everyone else.

'You think so?' she queried, in answer to his comment.

'Yes, why, do you really *always* want to know?' he returned.

'Sometimes not,' she admitted. 'But I'd like to with these ones. My mind can't make the leap to see them as happy, healthy toddlers, even though so often these days they do reach that point, and you'd never know, by the time they hit two or three, that they were premature.'

'Maybe the parents will send some photos.'

'Have a feeling not, in this case. It might be months before they have their babies home, and this part of the process will seem so long ago, and something they just want to forget. Particularly since what Dr Swanson was grumbling about during the flight was right, in many ways. They probably shouldn't have taken that holiday, and it must be hurting them that they did, and this was the result.'

'Think we're about ready to go,' Finn said. 'Takes a while, doesn't it? It'll be getting on for midnight by the time we touch down in Teymouth.'

'Did you handle everything, by the way?' she had to ask. 'I didn't get a chance to ask before.'

'Forgot to plug in the power straight away,' he admitted. 'So we were running on battery longer than we should have been.'

'Not a crucial mistake.'

'Hate any kind of mistake. I was kicking myself. That mechanical glitch with the plane had us all distracted and doing things in the wrong order.'

'You shouldn't have told me,' she teased. 'You could have kept your slip-up to yourself, and I would never have known.'

'Yeah, but there's something about your eyes, unfortunately, Anna Brewster,' he told her lightly in reply. 'Are you an enchantress, or something? I'm starting to wonder. Because I have a feeling I couldn't lie to you if I tried.'

Anna laughed, then felt herself blushing, which she knew was exactly the reaction he'd intended. He was flirting with her, deliberately reminding her that she felt something when they were together, and that he knew it. She ought to resent it, bristle at it, for Kendra's sake, but for some reason she couldn't.

If she was an enchantress, he was a wizard or a warlock, entrancing her not with mystic spells but with his honesty, and he didn't stop at admitting to medical mistakes either…

She made the fatal error of trying to top his wicked remark. 'Of course you could!' she said. 'Just give it a bit of practice, and I'm sure you'll get it right.'

A gleam lit up his wicked dark eyes. 'Don't want to practise,' he said. 'I'd much rather give it to you straight, Anna. You're doing something to me, you know that? And I like it, an' I don't want it to go away.'

What did a sweet threat like that deserve in the way of a comeback? Something. Definitely. A big, fat, squashy put-down to freeze him off. So why was it that all she could manage was a weak nod of acknowledgement, another even darker blush and no coherent comment at all?

She thought about him all the way back in the plane, skimming over the darkening waves below in Bass Strait, and the rugged centre of Tasmania, where scarcely a light broke the thick black of night-time. And when he said goodbye to her at chilly Teymouth airport at a quarter to twelve, her voice stuck in her throat when she tried to reply.

CHAPTER FIVE

'ANNA. Hello, it's Finn.'

She almost said, I know, since his voice was unique and branded permanently into her mind, but changed it just in time to a half bland, half wary, 'Hello, Finn.'

Then she was tempted to add something even more betraying, but managed not to.

It's taken you long enough, was what she wanted to say, because it felt so inevitable and right that she was hearing his voice, addressed just to her, at last. She had been thinking about him in almost every spare moment for days, no matter how hard she'd tried to fight it.

She'd been thinking about Kendra, too. She'd even phoned her cousin earlier in the week, hoping it would be some kind of antidote to Finn's devastating effect on her, but it was an awkward conversation and hadn't really helped.

Kendra had apologised. 'I'm sorry about what I said at Christmas. I didn't mean it, it was just hormones.'

'That's fine, Kendra, I knew that. But…have you been in touch with Finn?'

A beat of silence, then, 'No, not yet.'

'I think you should,' Anna jumped in, almost before she'd heard the word 'no'.

'I told you, I'm not going to—' Kendra began.

'But don't you want to get the situation resolved?'

Anna herself had. She still did.

If there was even the slightest possibility of Finn and Kendra cementing their relationship, whether misguidedly for the sake of the baby, or because they discovered they really loved each other after whatever had split them up so quickly back in Melbourne, then she wanted to know about it. Soon! And if there wasn't that possibility...

If there wasn't, she tried to remind herself, then that still put Finn McConnell well out of bounds, because there was no way she was going to let herself fall for a womaniser who ducked his responsibilities. Surely there was no way! She definitely did not share Kendra's forgiving, boys-will-be-boys, let-him-have-his-freedom attitude.

'It's complicated, Anna, I've told you that,' Kendra said.

And that, as Anna had known before, was where she and Kendra parted company. It *wasn't* complicated!

'I've met him...worked with him for a couple of days two weeks ago, and we run into each other all the time at the station now,' she told her cousin. She hadn't mentioned the emergency trip to Fryerstown.

'Oh, how is he?'

She refused to be drawn. 'Contact him yourself if you want to know. You have his details, don't you?'

'Of course I do. Craig told me—he phoned me last week—but—'

'Kendra, he seems...'

Really, if she was any judge of character, not the sort of man who *would* duck his responsibilities, and that was what she was starting to feel as if she did not understand. He seemed like such a straightforward person, with pure and refreshingly simple ideas about honour and duty and commitment.

'Have you told him how you feel?' she pressed. 'Does he know you'd like his help, and his involvement?

Maybe he feels as if, by leaving Melbourne, you've shut him out, signalled that you're not interested and don't want to acknowledge that he's the baby's father.'

'You don't understand…'

'No, I don't, although I'm trying to. So hard! Why don't you come to Teymouth for a visit? You could stay with me. See him. Talk. Work something out. Soon, please!'

'I have to handle it in my own way,' Kendra had insisted stubbornly, and Anna had eventually ended the conversation, having felt that the situation had been more frustrating than ever.

I need some way to feel on firm ground about this, she had told herself, thinking about it afterwards. If Kendra and Finn had some big knock-down fight and decided they didn't want any more to do with each other, then that would be one thing…and I could accept that the man I…

She had hesitated, groping around in her mind for a way of putting it that hadn't sounded too frightening to her inner ear.

A man I could feel something for, she'd come up with, had once fathered a baby with my own cousin. On the other hand, if they found that they loved each other, I *know* I would…I'd have to be able to…forget completely about the effect he has on me.

The same effect he was having on her right now, on the phone, despite her repeated resolutions to keep her defences up.

'I wondered if you were busy tomorrow,' he said.

'Sounds like maybe I should arrange to be,' she speculated incautiously.

Damn! Where had that come from? She was never as blunt as that, not even with her brother. But, admit it, she was actually light-headed with relief that Finn had phoned at last, had made a concrete attempt to do something about all the unacknowledged yet unmistakable chemistry that had exploded between them.

She had pretended to herself and to him that she was resistant, but she probably hadn't pretended very well. At work, some of the other paramedics were starting to talk, or to rib the two of them, with varying degrees of crudity, about their relationship. Everyone clearly assumed that they were having an affair, or at least teetering on the brink of one.

There hadn't been any concrete evidence, Anna considered.

She also told herself that she was pleased he wasn't making any moves on her…and some of the time she even meant it…but it was maddening and confusing, too. If he wasn't interested, what was the source of that *atmosphere*? It definitely wasn't coming from her.

Well, not just from her, she amended in her more honest moments.

They hadn't been rostered together since those first two days. Steve Quick had returned from Queensland in time to pick up his place on the roster again, and Finn had been moved into road duties, which was where any new recruit would normally begin. In any case, all the flight paramedics returned to road duty for regular blocks of time every few months in order to keep current with skills that were more frequently called upon on the ground.

Before this, Steve and Finn had made another triangular journey between Teymouth, Fryerstown and Melbourne to transfer Matthew's and Ashley's mother to Melbourne, so that she could be with her babies. In the roomy Beechcraft plane, they had been able to take the babies' father as well.

With the way their rosters had chanced to work out, however, Finn and Anna had still seen each other often.

In a job like this, everyone spent extensive though erratically timed stretches hanging around at headquarters. You could catch up on sleep or reading or television. Sometimes there were students or observers who had questions or needed a tour. There was administrative work to be done, report details to be completed. Some people pored over their pay-slips and suspiciously checked the calculations on their overtime. Often, however, groups of paramedics and junior ambulance officers simply gathered in the staffroom at meal and snack times to eat and talk.

And it had to be those times which had people grinning and speculating about herself and Finn, Anna had decided. She would find him sliding a piping hot mug of tea across to her at the big table in the staffroom when he hadn't even asked her if she wanted one. When he was telling an anecdote to two or three others, she'd look across to find that his dark gaze was on her.

And though, on occasion, she was ostensibly reading a book or the newspaper, or watching something on television, she'd suddenly hear herself adding something to the conversation and would realise, as several pairs of eyes focused in her direction, that she hadn't taken in a word of what she had been reading or watching for the past five minutes.

'If you're listening anyway, come and join us, Anna,' Ron or Matt or Louise would say.

Finn always stayed silent, never added his voice to the invitation. He would be studying his fingers, or staring into space with his coffee-mug to his lips, maybe chewing on some take-away Chinese, as if it didn't matter to him in the slightest whether she joined them or not.

But then, as she moved from the grey lounging chairs to the big white laminate table, she would see a little glow in his eyes. They would remain on her for just a moment, and if the chairs weren't arranged right, or if there wasn't a space, he would be the one to quietly shift so that it seemed natural for her to sit beside him.

Then, oh, then it would start. She would be aware of him every time he moved. She'd hear the soft slip of his shirt fabric against his skin as a shoulder shifted. She'd feel the warmth of his thigh, even though it wasn't in contact with hers at all.

If he had to move, she'd hear an apology. 'Sorry, Anna, shift your chair a bit, could you?' It would sound more like a line of seduction in that dark voice of his, with its twisted vowels and thick letter r. She'd feel the colour and heat flooding into her face for no reason at all, and would have to hide behind another mouthful of her meal.

Sometimes there would be a paging announcement, 'Crew to car 118, please, priority one.' And Finn and Diane or Finn and Mark would grimace briefly and get up from the table, perhaps gulping some last mouthfuls of coffee as they went.

'See you later, guys,' someone would say, and Anna would echo it and hear the way her voice didn't sounded quite natural. Too offhand, or too high-pitched.

After they had gone the convivial gathering somehow wouldn't be the same. The spark would be gone. Over the next ten minutes, she'd have to firmly stop herself from turning her head when she heard footsteps coming along the corridor, in case the call-out had been a false-alarm or in case a crew already on the road had been closer and had taken the job instead.

Sometimes, her head would turn anyway then turn back, and she knew that anyone who was watching her would be able to read the disappointment. She would end up gulping the rest of her tea and slinking back to the television chairs, trying to pretend to herself and to everyone else that Finn's absence wasn't the thing that had sent her away.

But she knew she was often an easy person to read. No wonder people teased them.

Now, at the other end of the phone, he laughed at her blunt words. They didn't seem to have put him off in the slightest. '*Arrange* to be busy? You really know how to flatter a man, don't you?'

'Finn—'

'Listen, Anna,' he said, and the sincerity that enriched his voice intrigued her and kept her silent. She wanted to hear what sort of a construction he was going to put on all this—their attraction, her wariness, his slowness to act over the past two weeks and more. 'Let's cut to the heart of this, shall we?' he went on. 'We're hugely attracted to each other.'

The erratic Scottish accent kicked in and made the word 'hugely' sound like something delicious and very decadent to eat.

'Please, admit it,' he said. 'It's been that way from the beginning. It's not a disease or a sin. I know…' He hesitated. 'That you have…or you think you have…some reason for not trusting me, or something. That's why I haven't jumped into this like the hothead I want to be when it comes to you.'

'I—'

'No, I'm not asking for an explanation, a'right?

Maybe you don't even have one. All I'm asking for is a chance to prove that, whatever it is, it's wrong. I've held off in case it all went away, in case you gave me a reason to stop feeling like this about you, but it hasn't gone away, and—' He broke off. 'Come to the beach with me tomorrow. Could you do that? Bring your open mind with you, leave everything else behind, and let's see where we end up.'

Of course, she said yes, and she honestly didn't know whether it was because of what he'd said, the honest arguments he'd used or the voice he'd said it in. She couldn't really claim he hadn't given her a chance to say no. But from the moment she'd heard his voice, that had never been a genuine option. Oh, she had known she was going to agree to whatever he proposed.

He picked her up the next morning at half past nine, wearing casual black shorts and an open-necked knit shirt with a subtle grey and green pattern. He was driving a lovingly restored and maintained classic yellow F J Holden, which was definitely not the vehicle he'd brought to work each day for the past two and a half weeks.

Anna inspected it in the driveway, and her landlady's young teenage son came down and inspected it, too, goggle-eyed with admiration. Finn had to exercise some tact in order to prise fourteen-year-old Tom away from the car, over whose waxed and polished paintwork he was running loving and reverent hands.

'You're a god, Finn,' Anna teased him as they drove away. She felt much more relaxed than she had expected to be, and the reasons for it were simple.

First, his failure to act on their sizzling attraction over the past two weeks had generated huge tension within her, which was now released. Second, she'd made a decision this morning. At some point today, when the timing felt right, she was going to talk to him about Kendra, tell him that she was Kendra's cousin, find out his perspective on the situation and take it from there.

Until then she was going to do as he had asked and give him the benefit of the doubt, keep an open mind, because there was no sense in spending any time with him at all if she did nothing but bristle with tension.

Setting all this out clearly in her mind felt good, an exertion of mastery and control, at last, over a situation she hadn't been in control of from the beginning.

'I don't use this vehicle for day-to-day commuting,' Finn explained as they turned out of Anna's street.

She rented a one-bedroom granny flat attached to a very pleasant house in West Teymouth. Her landlady was divorced with one child left at home, and the arrangement suited all of them. Judy Lawton could go out at night when Anna wasn't working, without Tom feeling as if he was being subjected to the indignity of a babysitter, and it meant that Anna got to live in a tranquil residential part of Teymouth, close to some wonderful parks, which she couldn't otherwise have afforded.

'Did you have to bring two cars across Bass Strait on the *Spirit of Tasmania*, then?' she asked, in answer to Finn's comment. The large car and passenger ferry plied the strait in each direction several times a week, linking Tasmania with the mainland.

'No, I picked the Toyota up a few weeks ago when I first got here,' he answered. 'Used car prices have dropped over the past couple of years, even though I suppose it's still an extravagance to run two vehicles.'

'This isn't a vehicle,' she told him. 'It's an entire lifestyle.'

He laughed, pleased. 'Someone who understands!'

Oh, she couldn't help it, she just grinned at him, feeling as if they shared some magic knowledge that nobody else had. This was making her dizzy, helpless. She'd never known anything like it, and the speed with which it was happening both frightened and delighted her.

Today, wearing a matching set of shorts and vest top in Wedgwood blue instead of uniform trousers and shirt, far away from the busy ambulance headquarters and from Fryerstown and the sombre, unsettling effect it always had on her mood, Anna had faith—faith that she didn't need to question the radiant connection between herself and Finn. It felt right, and therefore it had to be right, and nothing and no one else mattered.

Wriggling deep into the newly upholstered seat, which felt cool against her bare legs, she asked, 'Where are we going?'

'Putting your destiny in my hands?'

'I'm feeling sufficiently crazy today.'

'I'm glad about that.' He glanced across at her, his hands light on the steering-wheel and his dark eyes glinting with naked fire. Then he returned to her question. 'I thought we'd head for the east coast. Takes an hour and a half, according to my map, which makes it closer to two in this old friend. Is that too far for you?'

'No, I like driving. How does that saying go? It is better to travel than to arrive.'

'I was thinking that—or something very similar—just the other day.'

Another glance, smoky and thoughtful this time, made both her statement and his into something significant.

'I like driving, too,' he went on. 'Frees your thoughts. And this scenery's all new to me.'

'I've only been over to this part of the coast once myself, with some friends, and that time we went by the

other route. My parents take their holidays a lot further
south.'

'When we get there, I thought we'd just pick a beach,
preferably deserted, and swim and walk and eat.'

'Eat what? If the beach is deserted there won't be a
kiosk.'

'I packed a picnic,' he said.

'Finn! You should have told me to bring something.'

'As I remember, I specially instructed you to bring
absolutely nothing.'

'Except my swimsuit and a towel, I assumed.' She
had a small leather backpack at her feet containing these
items, as well as hat, sunscreen and sunglasses.

'As to your swimsuit, it depends on how deserted the
beach is, doesn't it?' The lazy, suggestive drawl made
it quite apparent what he meant.

She almost gasped as an image flooded into her mind
of Finn's strong body, naked in the foaming waves,
streaming with water and glinting in the sun, while she
swam and rolled beside him, the cold caress of the water
buffing her skin into tingling life.

Oh, she wouldn't dare, no matter how deserted the
beach!

He was laughing again. 'You're not shocked?'

'I'm not a prude. I've done it before.'

'After dark, in a pool, with female friends,' he
guessed.

'Yes, exactly. Different if it's an open beach in broad
daylight, with—'

'Who says it will still be daylight by then?'

'How long are we staying?'

'However long you like.'

'I'm working tomorrow.'

'I'm not. I'll tuck you up in a couple of nice dry

towels and you can sleep in the car on the way home while I drive. When we get there I'll scoop you up in my arms—you'll have given me your key earlier—carry you inside and nestle you into your soft white bed. And then I'll—'

'My quilt cover is blue and green and gold, with sheets to match,' she came in quickly.

'Don't mess my head up with irrelevant details, woman!'

'I think you're the one who's messing up my head,' she muttered, knowing he would hear.

'Maybe that's the idea,' he suggested softly.

They drove in silence for a while, and Anna pretended to watch the scenery. It wasn't a perfect day. The temperature was mild but the sky was overcast, threatening to drizzle. And that only went to prove how unlikely it was that her image of the two of them swimming naked together would be realised, because that fantasy had contained a perfect arc of blue sky and brilliant, glorious sunshine.

'But, you know, I like it overcast this way,' Finn said two hours later.

They'd had a good talk in the car, and Anna had seen a different Finn from the one who sat at the big table in the staffroom yarning and ribbing the other paramedics. He had talked about his serious battle with leukaemia fifteen years ago, and didn't have to spell out for her the way his illness had moulded him as a man.

Then, when she'd tried to put into words a rather cloudy perception that they'd both come through periods of *poisoning* in their lives—his chemotherapy, her childhood in Fryerstown—he had known what she meant.

'Isn't there some saying about that?' he'd said. 'What

doesn't kill me makes me strong, or something. I've always thought that was true.'

Now they had found a long sweep of beach between St. Mary's and Bicheno, accessible only by a dirt track and then a muscle-knotting trek across the deep, drifted dunes. Some of the threatened rain had fallen, just enough to dapple and dampen the sand. Enough, too, to discourage most summer beach-goers. The stretch of sand was deserted apart from a handful of surfers way up the other end. They must have found a different access point, because there were no cars parked near Finn's.

In a backpack larger than Anna's, he carried the picnic, and he had a towel slung around his neck. They had both put on sunscreen back at the car.

'To ensure that we won't see a single ray of horrible, nasty sunshine all day,' Finn said.

'Oh, absolutely,' Anna agreed. 'Wouldn't want sun.'

'Sun is so *obvious*. I mean, everyone wants sun, and all it does is bring the teeming masses crowding onto the beach.'

And they discovered after a while that it was true. Who did need sun? The misty grey sky was what made it special, painting the landscape of sea and sand and sky with the subtlest and coolest of colours.

They ate straight away, spreading out towels on the sand in a little hollow in the lee of the dunes. The picnic Finn had provided was eccentric and spontaneous. Some tubs of fruit yoghurt. A packet of smoked salmon and one of cream cheese. Cracker biscuits, bread rolls, a whole head of oakleaf lettuce. A cold anchovy pizza, with two slices missing. Two bottles of beer, one bottle of cider and some mineral water mixed with juice. A blob of butter in a plastic container and a jar of strawberry jam.

'Did you shop for this specially, or was it just what you happened to have in the house?' Anna had to ask.

'Uh…a bit of both,' he confessed. 'Is it revolting?'

'That depends. How old is the pizza?'

'Nine o'clock last night, after I got off work late. Wasn't as hungry as I thought.'

'In the fridge overnight?'

'Promise! Anchovy. Goes with the seafood theme, see.' He pointed at the smoked salmon.

'So which is the main course, then, and which is the hors d'oeuvre?'

'Suit yourself.'

Perhaps it shouldn't have been delicious but it was, eaten, in the end, in no order at all. Each flavour seemed somehow stronger and tangier today, with the sea air sharpening their appetites and their thirst. Then they left their backpacks on the sand and went for a walk the length of the beach, splashing up to their ankles in the cold, salty water, both of them happy to let the thunder and hiss of the waves drown the need for conversation.

A faint mist hung in the air over the water and the cool beige sand, and somehow the dullness of the day made the irregular line of foam, as each wave slid up the sand, glow with a pure, almost iridescent white. The air was cool and fresh and filled with ozone and the clean smell of the sea.

On the way back, Finn took Anna's hand and she let him, and again they didn't speak, which gave her all the time in the world to realise, This is important. Already. It's not just a little twenty-four-hour lust virus that's going to be over when I wake up tomorrow. He makes me laugh. That silly picnic! He makes me think and feel. He makes me... Oh, help!

Suddenly, he had pulled her out of these crucial thoughts.

Run and jump in the sand dunes with him until I'm breathless and happy and my hair and clothes are full of the stuff...! 'Finn!' she shrieked aloud.

It didn't take Anna long to catch the mood, and it was wonderful, ten minutes of pure exhilaration. They chased each other back to the wandering pathway which ran from the rutted parking area to the beach, zigzagging up and down the dunes. Their flying feet sent cold sand bulldozing downwards as it tickled and hugged their legs.

Running just ahead of Finn, as they took a short cut towards the path, Anna was laughing too hard to take any notice of where her feet fell, and didn't realise the significance of the patch of charcoal and ash that fanned out across the sand and darkened it to a bluish grey just at this point. Vaguely, she knew that someone must have had a fire here a few weeks ago.

Then her instep pressed down hard on something sharp and painful, and she limped and staggered for a few more paces through the sand until she half fell to a sitting position.

'What's wrong?' Finn said, slowing to a breathless halt beside her.

'I trod on something...'

'Oh, hell, there's broken glass. Some idiots have had a drinking session here and entertained themselves by smashing the bottles afterwards. Look!' He swore again. 'It's everywhere!'

They both saw it now—chunks and splinters of brown

glass on the surface of the sand and half buried beneath it, mingled with the lumps of charcoal.

Anna bent her knee up, twisted her foot and looked at her instep. It was running with blood, getting mixed with the sand encrusted on her feet and making it red and sticky.

'Is the glass still in there?' Finn stepped carefully towards her and dropped to the sand.

He picked up several more shards of broken beer bottle and put them in a pile where they wouldn't be a danger to their bare limbs.

Anna began to inspect her foot, but the reddening sand made it hard to see. Finn pulled a wad of clean tissues from the back pocket of his black shorts, took her foot in the warm curve of his palm and began to wipe the sand away. Anna was distracted by the sober line of his brows and the silken texture of his eyelids as he looked down. She hardly felt the cut for a long moment, just wanted to reach out and explore his face with her fingers.

But the blood kept coming, and now they could both see the clean, slightly curved edges of the cut.

He pressed gently. It hurt, but not too sharply. 'Doesn't feel to me like there's anything in there,' he said. 'How does it feel from your end?'

Fabulous! Keep stroking my foot like that with the ball of your thumb. I don't think you've even noticed you're doing it...

'Nothing,' she agreed in a thin voice that was almost a gasp. 'I don't think it's too deep.'

Wishful thinking? The last thing she wanted was to be compelled to sidetrack from this heart-stopping day in favour of a trip to Casualty in St Helen's for some stitches.

Fortunately, Finn agreed. He stopped that hypnotic caress, gently and carefully pulled the edges of the cut apart with his thumbs just enough to gauge its depth, then pressed them together again and said, 'I've got a first aid kit in the car. I think that'll cover it.'

'Good.'

'But we can go home, if you like.'

'No!'

He didn't say anything, but she could read the gladness in his body as he slid her foot back onto the sand, keeping the cut clear of the dry grains.

'Don't move!' he told her, and she watched him as he made his way crookedly across the spinifex-covered dunes to the car. His legs were strong and tanned and every bit as hairy as a good man's legs should be.

He was back with the items he needed from the first-aid kit in five minutes, and it was a simple matter to brush the dry sand off and dress the cut with antiseptic ointment and several strips of adhesive bandage.

'But I won't be able to swim,' she realised aloud. 'Or those plasters will come straight off and the sand and water will open up the cut.'

'Don't worry, I'll keep you company on the sand.'

'No, you won't,' she retorted. 'You can swim for me! Hope you brought your togs.'

'Yes, in the end. Fortunately,' he added, watching the parking area. 'It was a tough decision, but looks like I made the right choice.'

Another car had just pulled up next to Finn's—an old green station wagon with a light fibreglass surfboard strapped to the top. A rather scruffy man got out, followed by two children, a boy and a girl, aged about seven and four. The kids were already dressed in swimming gear, and carried balled-up towels, clutching them awkwardly in the crooks of their arms.

The man took no notice of them once they were out of the car. He was unstrapping his surfboard from the roof-rack and inspecting it, running his hands over its surface.

The children asked him something, and he pointed at the track leading to the beach. From where they stood in the lee of the dunes, the children wouldn't have been able to see the water. They set off in the right direction while the man stripped naked beside the car and began to put on a sleek, knee-length black wetsuit then zipped it up to his neck.

'Oops,' Finn said. 'Has he seen us?'

'Maybe he doesn't care.'

'That's a surfer's body, if ever I saw one.'

As the man was quickly decent in his wetsuit, they kept looking at him. His skin, during the brief seconds of nakedness, had come in three distinct shades—dark tan on face and below elbows and knees where the wet-suit stopped, lighter tan on his torso because on hot days he obviously surfed only in board shorts, and pallid white from waist to thighs.

The man fiddled about some more, then checked and locked the car. The children must be out of his sight now, but he hadn't taken any notice. They had become distracted by the inviting shapes of the dunes, and started to do what Anna and Finn had done earlier—lots of run-ning and jumping and shrieking, on the opposite side of the sandy path from where Finn and Anna still sat.

'Is it safe over there, do you think?' Anna asked.

'I'd better warn their dad,' Finn agreed. 'Can't see any glass from here but, then, we didn't notice this lot until we got close to it.'

He set off to intercept the surfer, who was now on his way to the beach, with his board tucked under his arm.

Anna began to follow Finn, carrying an empty plastic container left over from lunch and picking up pieces of glass as she went. Probably silly to bother. It would take hours of systematically combing the sand to find all of it, but every little bit helped.

'Clean Up Australia' day was coming in early March. Perhaps she could phone the nearest Scout troop and suggest they make the glass their project this year.

Finn had reached the children's father, and was talking and gesturing. Anna wasn't yet quite close enough to hear his words, but she heard the surfer yell, 'Kids, watch where you jump, OK? This man says there's broken glass. I'm going to catch some waves. You know where I'll be if you need me.'

He thanked Finn politely, then continued his way towards the beach, raising his head to scrutinise the surf. Anna caught up to Finn, who shrugged at her. They didn't need to voice their scepticism aloud. Was a casual warning like that enough for two rather young children? No, it wasn't.

The surfer hadn't even reached the tide line when Anna and Finn saw that the younger child, the girl, was crying and hobbling. Her brother had his arm around her and they were picking their way across the sand-hills toward the beach.

'Dad? Dad!' the boy yelled. 'Kimberley's cut her foot! *Dad!*' He cupped his hands around his mouth.

Their father heard and turned, began to walk reluctantly back, then quickened his pace as the boy repeated even louder, *'Kimberley's cut her foot!'*

Halfway up the beach he dropped his board and began to run, and Anna and Finn, who were making their way towards the two children as well, heard him start to swear. The three adults reached the two children at the same time.

'Oh, hell, you weren't wrong about the glass, were you?' the surfer groaned.

'I cut my own foot a few minutes earlier,' Anna said.

'It hurts,' Kimberley whimpered.

'Have you got two bandages, then?' her father demanded of Anna.

'In the car,' Finn said. 'I'll be back in a minute, a'right?'

'Thanks, mate. Kimberley, sit down, OK? No! Not there! There's more glass!'

The sudden shout frightened the girl and her sobs freshened, although Anna could tell that her father was more alarmed than angry. Remorseful, too.

'This is a stuff-up,' he muttered, as he cleared a safe patch for the girl to sit down. 'Jamie, check if there's any more glass around and, for heaven's sake, watch your own feet. That'd be the last thing we need! What in hell made me think I'd get any surfing in?'

He was still cursing himself, the drunken bottle-smashers and life in general when Finn got back. Kimberley had stopped crying, and Jamie looked pensive and subdued and not very happy.

During Finn's absence, Anna had cleaned the sand from the cut with the corner of Kimberley's towel and had looked at it carefully. Like hers, it wasn't too deep, but she could see that there was a splinter of glass left in it, and it was in a more awkward position, too, slicing up from the ball of the foot to the space between the first and second toes. Fortunately, Finn had brought the whole kit with him this time.

'In case there's still glass in it,' he said.

'There is,' Anna confirmed.

He handed her the tweezers and said, 'I'll defer to your finer fingers.' The child's father seemed to have no desire to tackle the ugly splinter himself.

Kimberley made a remarkably good patient. Anna soon had the glass fragment out, and Finn was preparing a more elaborate dressing because simple adhesive bandages would never hold in such an awkward spot. It was the children's father who needed their best bedside manner.

'Donna's going to murder me!' he was saying. 'It's hopeless! I have them one weekend a month, and every bloody time I do something wrong. Last time I ironed a dirty great scorch mark on Kimberley's party dress. Now it's this. My ex thinks I'm just an idiot—and I am. Jeez, you'd think I'd know by now that you can't turn your back for a minute! But it's hard when you're not with them all that often. You forget how it is. You're not really part of their lives. You're not in the habit of watching out for their safety and putting them first. You just *forget*!'

The two children were silent and large-eyed through all this, as if the flood of complex and very adult emotions was overwhelming for them.

When the cut was dressed, the dad—he'd told Finn and Anna that his name was Anthony—said to his children, 'Wait here, OK?' Then he loped back to the car, rummaged about on the floor of the front seat for a minute and returned.

'You didn't have to wait,' he told Anna and Finn.

'Well…'

'Thanks a million, by the way. Are you doctors, or something?'

'Paramedics,' Finn answered.

'Right…'

'Ambulance officers,' Anna clarified.

'Oh, OK.' His brow cleared. 'Then I guess you would know a bit about first aid.' He was obviously one of the many people who didn't realise just how highly qualified the paramedics of the Tasmanian Ambulance Service were.

Anthony bent down to his little girl and began to pull something colourful up over her foot. An old plastic bread bag, Anna saw. He secured it in place with a thick rubber band and said cheerfully, 'There! Bet you thought we'd have to go home, didn't you, kids? Well, we don't, see! We're going to dig in the sand instead. Might paddle a bit. Jamie can jump some waves. Then we'll stop off and get ice creams on the way home. We're gong to have a great afternoon!'

It was like the sun coming out, which it was starting to look as if it might actually do. The children dropped their cloaks of timidity and fear, as if suddenly discovering that they hadn't done anything wrong after all, as they'd obviously thought, and Finn and Anna realised that the little part-time family was going to be all right.

A few minutes later, after more thanks from Anthony and echoes from the children, the three of them were down near the tide line digging all sorts of wonderful channels and moats, castles and tunnels. Anthony had his wetsuit pulled down, with the arms tied around his waist, and he was directing Jamie to dig towards the incoming waves. Jamie's shouts of excitement carried all the way up to the dunes.

Anna and Finn were collecting their gear, ready to leave. Despite the happy outcome for Kimberley and her brother, the earlier mood of misty solitude on the beach was spoiled now. Anna's foot throbbed, and she and Finn didn't have a plastic bread bag and a rubber band to waterproof it with. She had to try and keep up on her toes as she walked and Finn had just picked up several more lethal-looking pieces of glass.

'It's after three,' he said. 'Feel like finding a café or something, and then heading back? I'm assuming you're no longer up for that naked moonlight swim we've both been looking forward to all day.'

'That was only ever in your dreams, Finn,' she told him.

He didn't let her get away with it. 'Just in *my* dreams, eh? I don't think so…'

She fought against a blush, and lost. Tossed her head instead, and stalked off so that he wouldn't see. Behind her, she could almost hear his smug satisfaction in the rhythm of his footsteps. He caught up to her a moment later, and she half expected him to push the point…or pull her into his arms. He did neither.

Instead, he said thoughtfully and quite fervently, 'Gee, I hope I'm never in that position!'

'What position?'

'Part-time dad. Two nights out of fourteen, or even twenty-eight, like Anthony. Kid, or kids, plonked in my car at six on a Friday evening, to be returned by dinnertime on Sunday night, preferably still in one piece, thank you very much. I mean, an awful lot of people make it work, and that's great. My hat's off to them. They're heroes, the lot of them, mums, dads and kids. But…'

He shook his head.

'I'm no saint,' he went on. 'I've had my share of relationships. A couple of them serious. Some a big mistake. But I can say one thing. I've always been damned careful not to father a child.'

The words washed over Anna like a bucket of cold water.

He's lying. That was her first outraged thought.

Then she arrived at the truth, and knew she wasn't wrong. Finn had spoken so confidently, his opinion as usual straightforward and his conscience clear and unclouded.

Oh, my Lord! Kendra hasn't told him she's pregnant.

That's what this is all about. That's why he's acting as if he's a free agent in the way he and I respond to each other. That's why, intuitively, I haven't been able to condemn him the way I've tried to. It's why he's never mentioned her, and why Kendra herself has been so evasive and strange, with all that talk about not pressing a man.

He doesn't know.

CHAPTER SIX

ANNA was stunned by the realisation, and she was silent, her thoughts churning, as they bumped carefully along the rutted track and back to the main road in Finn's car.

Kendra hadn't told him.

Their relationship had been short-lived. Anna thought back and tried to pick some simple facts out of Kendra's vague and highly coloured narrative. Perhaps it was only the one time that they'd slept together. Then, as far as Finn was concerned, the relationship had ended, Kendra had left Melbourne... Thinking back, Anna had the impression she had kept up a closer contact with Craig.

Yes, because she doesn't *want* Finn to know. Not until the baby is born. And she's scared she'll betray the truth if she talks to him on the phone. She must think he'll be more interested after the birth, when his child is a reality and when Kendra herself has that gorgeous figure of hers back again. Her skin will probably clear up, too. That's it. That's why she's hiding away in Fryerstown. It's not just because she's broke. She wants to give it her best shot with Finn. She really wants him...

And meanwhile Finn could make innocent, idealistic speeches about not fathering a child in a casual relationship because he hated the idea of part-time fatherhood, unaware that there *was* a child of his loins in the world, now less than three months shy of being born.

I have to think. I have to work out what this means for *me*.

Was that selfish? Perhaps. That was irrelevant. At the

moment, it was a matter of emotional survival. Only now did she realise how deep her feelings went. She was twenty-eight years old. She'd had boyfriends. Two at art school. One of the trainee paramedics in Hobart, and another paramedic, here in Teymouth, early last year.

She and Brenton had only gone out together for a couple of months. Working together, it had been awkward and they'd both soon agreed that the relationship hadn't been going anywhere. It had been best to end it before things had got ugly and it had threatened their professional dealings with each other.

Brenton had left the service a few months later, to follow his second love of fine wood-working full time. She had heard he was about to get married.

But neither Brenton nor the others had touched her heart and soul like Finn did. In his case, she didn't care that they worked together, found herself shrugging at the potential risks. She had been so hostile towards him at first, and it was incredible how quickly that had broken down, how quickly she had come to feel that she knew him, and that he wasn't the kind of man she'd conjured up in her imagination—the uncaring father of Kendra's coming child.

Because he didn't know.

'You're quiet,' he said, after a silence whose length she couldn't measure.

Where were they? Coming into the tiny town of Kerry Creek already, nearly halfway home.

'Feeling sleepy?' he wanted to know.

'No, I'm fine.'

'Foot hurting, then?'

'Nothing like that.'

'Then what?'

'I...have a headache.' Extremely feeble, but the best Anna could come up with.

'We'll have some tea, if there's a café here. That'll help. And you can take some tablets. There are some in the kit.'

'It's earning its keep today,' she joked thinly.

'It is,' he agreed.

He was taking the headache at face value, then.

Well, he would, she quickly decided. As she'd observed before, he was a straightforward man, one who wore his virtues—honesty and kindness, for example—easily and openly and without fuss or self-aggrandisement. Precious virtues, they were, too, and much more rare than they should be. It hadn't taken her long to know all this about him. The only jarring note was struck by what she had thought she knew about his attitude to Kendra, and now this contradiction was cleared away.

Oh, sweet heaven, I'm in love with him! I'm not just teetering on the brink. I dived in days ago.

'Here we go,' Finn said, coming to a halt outside an old stone cottage set a little way back from the main street behind a white picket fence. He got out of the car, strode closer and studied it for half a minute, then came back to her, opened the passenger door for her and took her elbow. 'This place looks a'right, d'you think?'

The cut foot was throbbing, and she wasn't quite as steady as usual as she climbed from the car.

'Lace curtains, and little rosebuds in vases on the tables,' he went on, bending to hold her steady. 'Really cute, it is.'

He had her on her feet now, and was looking into her face, his eyes warm and glinting with mischief and...something else. Something important.

'Finn, you hate places like this!' Anna laughed, almost in tears at the same time. Her heart was turning over

She loved him, and he cared about her, she was almost sure of it. It wasn't just a man's short-lived physical need. He would be handling this very differently if it was just that. He wouldn't have frozen like this, with the two of them sandwiched in the space between the seat and the open car door.

'Eh, yes, I always feel as though I'm going to…knock something over with my elbow,' he was saying, as if it had all been important when he'd started the sentence but was getting less and less so with every word. 'But I can…smell the scones baking…and…'

They stood together, both motionless. His face was inches away. He watched her mouth with his dark eyes and she watched those eyes until she couldn't bear it any longer. She let her lashes and her lids sweep down as a tiny sound vibrated in her throat and caught there, a whimper of need that was almost painful.

He was hesitant. They both were. Almost clumsy about it, too. Which side was he going to angle his head? Where did their noses belong? It all happened very slowly, so that her breath was fluttery and shallow in anticipation, and it felt as if the world had stopped turning.

But finally their mouths met perfectly, soft and clinging and tender and hungry. He had one hand resting loosely on her bare arm. She clutched a handful of his shirt fabric near the waist, scrunching it up so that the heel of her hand nudged against silky, warm skin.

The fingers of their other hands tangled together. He took a small step forward and his thigh touched hers, pushing her legs apart a little and shoring her up at the same time. Another tiny step brought his stomach against her ribs and the soft press of her breasts against his chest.

They tasted each other, lingered a little more, then very slowly let each other go.

Anna felt dizzy, and the whole universe had gone soft at the edges. Neither of them needed to speak. They both knew that ending the kiss now, so soon, meant only that they would take it up again later, when they were alone.

The sense of magic and anticipation was all-consuming. The air itself seemed to glow. Anna's chest was tight and there was a heavy fullness deep inside her. It ached. Not pain, but tingling awareness and need. It made her want to laugh and sing.

Finn was laughing already. His fingers were still knotted with hers as he turned towards the café and nudged the car door shut behind him with his hip. She took three hobbling steps and caught up to him, and his arms dropped around her shoulders and pulled her into the hollow between his chest and upper arm.

'How did I know it would feel this good, eh?' he murmured. 'How did I know?'

She couldn't answer, just had to smile and look at him. Everything she felt reflected back at her from his eyes, too.

They ordered Devonshire teas and he made her take two headache tablets, which she did because she was vaguely aware that she did have a throbbing pain at the back of her head somewhere. It might have hurt if she'd been able to think about it.

But all she could think about was him, and they were openly and rapturously lost in each other as they ate and drank and talked, and then as they drove again.

At Anna's flat, Judy and her son didn't seem to be home. The weather was clearing. It must have rained more here than on the east coast, because the ground was wet and the air had that fresh, tangy smell of eucalyptus and earth, but now the sun had broken through in several places and was bringing out the green of trees and grass so that they glowed richly in the golden evening light. It was almost seven o'clock.

It was so obvious Finn was coming in and they were spending the evening together that she didn't even bother to ask. Inside her flat, he seemed too large at first, as he prowled around looking at some of her drawings, mounted on the wall. She had to stifle the urge to clear a space for him—push the coffee-table back against the wall and take half the cushions off the couch, or something. The need soon passed.

He accepted a beer, she poured herself a glass of white wine and they discussed dinner possibilities lazily as they drank. The matter didn't seem at all important. Anna privately felt that she probably wouldn't even be able to concentrate on a take-away restaurant menu long enough to choose anything.

'I have pasta and some jars of sauce,' she offered vaguely in the end.

'Sounds great,' he said, as if he didn't care in the slightest either.

She filled a saucepan with water to boil, emptied the first jar of sauce she found into a second saucepan and said, 'There! Done!' Then she turned away from the stove, to find him laughing at her as he leaned against the humming fridge.

'What?' she demanded.

'Nothing,' he answered, with the laugh still colouring his voice, and she didn't need him to tell her that he wanted her in his arms.

She went to him, hardly able to believe that something

could feel so right and yet so dangerously sensual at the same time. She'd always somehow assumed that love would feel like slipping into a comfortable pair of old slippers.

Instead, it was… Well, maybe they were slippers, but they were slippers of the hand-made, Italian leather, crystal-beaded moccasin variety, fitting with a soft caress like a second skin but utterly luxurious and perfectly worked at the same time.

In short, it was heaven.

He was still smiling as he gathered her against him. 'Anna…' Her name was like melting chocolate in his mouth.

This time he kissed her properly, his mouth coming down slowly onto hers with a sensual precision that had her heart pounding as she waited for it. She was content to stay quiescent in his arms, to hang back and watch while he did all the work.

She was tired, almost drugged by the hours of fresh sea air and a little fuzzy from the effect of the wine on an empty stomach. Her limbs felt deliciously heavy and the hard warmth of his body supporting hers all along its length made her feel heavier still—a different kind of heaviness this time, a fullness deep inside her.

'Mmm, don't let me go,' she murmured against his mouth. 'Please, Finn!'

'I'm not planning to. Not until you tell me to.'

'Can't imagine…that I'll ever find the words…'

She closed her eyes. Sight was simply a distraction, the easiest and most ordinary of the senses. She wanted to sense him in every other way, without her eyes. He smelled of the sea, and of nutty soap and a tiny bit of sweat. He tasted of beer, too. Pleasantly so. It wasn't a drink she normally enjoyed herself, but on a man's mouth it could taste just right, a complicated blend of very male flavours.

He felt warm, soft in some places, hard in others. There was the resilient give of honed muscle cushioning her and supporting her where his arms wrapped around her body. There was the rigid bump and nudge of hips and aroused manhood against her swelling groin. There was the sheer sense of his solid bulk.

The only way she would ever topple this man would be if she caught him off guard. Something just felt right about that—that he was stronger than she was but would use that strength only to shield and support her, never to overpower or dominate.

Even the sounds they made together inflamed her need for him—those growling purrs of satisfaction in his throat, the gentle rasp of his lightly roughened chin and jaw against her cheek.

The pasta water came to the boil and then boiled half away before they stopped to add the packet of thin linguine, and it would have overcooked if she hadn't dragged her mouth from his kiss once more to say, 'I like it *al dente*.'

'You mean like this?' Deliberately, he caught her lower lip softly between his teeth, then licked away the minute sensation of pain with the tip of his tongue.

'I meant the linguine.'

'That means tongue-shaped, doesn't it?'

'Think so.'

'And *al dente* means "on the teeth". Or "chewy", I suppose. Very sensual, the Italians.'

'In my experience the Scots aren't bad either.'

'And how much experience *is* that, exactly? That you've had of Scotsmen, I mean.'

'Keep doing that…and that…for long enough and I'll be able to fill an encyclopaedia.'

By the time they got to the linguine it wasn't very *al dente*, but neither of them cared.

It was after ten when Finn reluctantly left, and Anna knew he would have stayed all night if she had given him the word. Oh, and that word almost burned her mouth with its eagerness to escape.

Stay. Please, stay, Finn.

She had to bite it back, fight it like a chocolate fiend fighting the sweet lure of Easter displays. The temptation badgered at her repeatedly. When he put down his coffee-cup. When he got to his feet. When he kissed her again. When the music on the CD player died to an expectant silence at just the right moment. When he said something hopeful and hinting about how it had chilled down outside now, although it was so cosy here in her flat.

Oh, she knew what he wanted, and he knew that she knew it.

Might as well just say it.

'I'm not going to, Finn.'

'Ah, well, greater powers of control than I have.' He had known exactly what she meant.

'Not *much* greater.'

'Good…'

'Don't kiss me again, because—'

'It would be the last straw? Even better!' He shaped himself to take her in his arms once more.

'I…mean it, Finn.'

'I know you do, gorgeous, and… Aagh!' He groaned. 'Can't believe I'm saying this! What kind of a man am I? Anna, I—respect—that! Hell, that was hard! Those words just didn't want to come out. Would you like me to take them back?' he offered hopefully.

'No, Finn. Yes…but, no. Not yet.'

They both laughed, and she added carefully, 'Sorry, mixed signals. Can't think tonight, and I *want* to, you see. You know, that cold-light-of-day thing? Morning after the night before?'

'I know,' he said. 'And I know it'll mean more that way when it does happen. And that's important, Anna. I want you to know that, a'right?'

'Yes…yes, oh, and I do.' She nodded, having to wrap her arms around herself in order not to wrap them around him instead and undo all the hard work of the past few minutes.

He left finally, and she stood in the doorway and watched him all the way to the car, then watched the car as far as she could see it down the street.

It was only once she had cleaned up their few dishes and made her preparations for bed that she was able to think, I started today planning to tell him I was Kendra's cousin, but everything has changed now. He doesn't know that he has any reason to think of Kendra ever again. He thinks we're both free and that all our problems are over.

It wasn't true. She knew that, almost as strongly and intuitively as she knew that she loved him, but tonight…the whole day…had been so perfect she just couldn't see the dark side at the moment. She had as much confidence and happiness and faith as Finn, and when she went to bed and to sleep at last, her dreams were glorious.

He phoned her the next evening, after she got home from work. Anna and Matt, driving car 118, had been quite busy today, with several call-outs, but none of them had been very dramatic.

There had been one unappealing idiot with stale alcohol on his breath and a broken toe. He had already made one ambulance trip to the hospital three days previously, two days after the break had happened, to be given strong painkillers—which he hadn't bothered to take, it turned out—and some instructions about rest and care.

Anna and Matt had had to tell him that there was nothing more to be done. He had been given the appropriate treatment the first time, his pain had not been an emergency and he had just been wasting their time.

There had been a collapse that had turned out to be a mild stroke, there had been an asthma attack and there had been another collapse of an elderly man at his home. They had quickly diagnosed this as being due to low blood sugar, which had been easily remedied. Then there had been a case of chest pain in a middle-aged man, who had been admitted to Teymouth Hospital for tests.

Finally, there was a road traffic accident in which no one was injured. Sometimes you couldn't trust an accident victim's claim that there was 'nothing wrong with me'. If you looked at their car and it was in tatters, you had to take such claims with a large pinch of salt and often exercise some tactful persuasion towards a ride to hospital 'just to check things out'.

People were often in shock, hyped up and distracted, and simply weren't aware of their injuries at first. All they could see was the expensive damage to their car. Internal bleeding was silent, and far less obvious than a crushed and twisted car body. But on today's accident scene Matt and Anna could trace the progression of the two moderately damaged vehicles. No sudden explosive halt over two or three metres, but a drawn out skid over about twenty-five metres, creating a much less jarring impact.

The three people involved claimed no injury. They seemed like sensible people and were relatively calm, and on the evidence Anna and Matt believed them.

On the phone to Finn, Anna vented her feelings a little about the man with the toe and described the new black skid marks now sketched on the concrete sides of the Wetherill Street overpass, but didn't need to go into any more detail about her day.

He didn't suggest getting together, and she appreciated that. He understood her need for breathing space. Perhaps he felt it, too. But it was good that he'd phoned. It gave her a warm feeling of hope and confidence and happiness, and he finished their casual conversation with, 'See you tomorrow. You're on at night, right?'

'Yep. I'm yawning already.'

'See you around seven, then.'

It left her feeling as if the whole world glowed.

Although they were both working the night-time roster, Finn and Anna were on different crews the following night. Anna was paired with Ron, while Finn himself was working with one of the service's most experienced paramedics, Diane McMahon.

Diane was a nice woman, a former nurse, married to an architect. They had two school-age children. She was hard-working and calm in a crisis, a jewel with every patient and a complete, ear-bashing motor-mouth at the wheel. Finn's hair stood on end at some of the curses and commentary she flung at other drivers, each word delivered through clenched teeth as she navigated the streets and the traffic with steely concentration.

He knew why she was like that. In fact, he had realised that she was a far better driver than she would have given herself credit for, but the driving, especially on a P1 call-out with full sirens and lights, wasn't her favourite part of the job. She had to get her mental adrenaline up in order to stay on top of, say, speeding the wrong way up Teymouth's busiest arterial road in peak-hour traffic, when startled motorists didn't always manage to veer out of the way as quickly as they should.

Unfortunately for Finn, understanding Diane's psychology on the issue and actually putting up with her driving style were two very different things. In the three weeks he'd worked in Teymouth, this would be the fourth shift he'd been paired with her.

Everyone had different ways of splitting up the driving and the patient care in the back of the car. Some people preferred to go 'job about'. Others liked it when one crew member drove for the whole of one shift, and did reports and patient care the next. The latter was what Diane preferred, and she seemed in no doubt that it was her turn at the wheel today. Finn didn't argue, but had to steel himself mentally for a long night of commentary.

He hoped the shift would be quiet, and his desire to avoid Diane's tirades wasn't the only reason. If things were quiet, he'd get to see Anna.

Ah, didn't that present some great pictures to his mind's eye! He loved the way she pulled her overalls down to her waist when she was relaxing, and used the sleeves to tie them there. Beneath the overalls, she'd be wearing some neat, close-fitting T-shirt in grey or navy or white. Her bare arms were so smooth and graceful, just like that long neck of hers. As for her breasts, softly moulded by the fabric of the T-shirt...

Tonight, if he did get the chance to see her dressed

like that, he knew he was going to torture himself by remembering how those rounded shapes had pressed against him on Saturday night.

At midnight, crews were permitted to bed down for the night, suggesting more appealing images. Anna in the early hours, for example, woken from sleep, all rumpled and warm. Anna curled up in a lounging chair at dawn, waking herself up with coffee, her fine hands wrapped around the mug to steal its heat. Anna, grumpy and growling, brushing her hair into submission then pulling it high, with her head ducked and her arms bent up behind her as she twisted a ring of colourful elastic around the thick mass to keep the ponytail in place.

Finn had to suppress a shudder of need, still thinking about Anna as Tony, from the departing day crew, brought him the drug book to sign for the morphine.

'You're driving 117 tonight, right? With Diane?' Tony said.

'Right.'

'Brought your earplugs?'

Everyone joked about Diane's tirades, even in her hearing, as now.

'Guys, I'm sorry, I just *have* to!' she said, backing out of the rear of vehicle 117, parked two metres away. She had understood the earplug comment at once. 'We need a couple of masks for the oxygen kit, Finn. Other than that, we're checked out and ready to go.'

'Let's hope we don't have to.'

'You can drive if you want to,' Diane offered. 'Only I haven't done it for four shifts now, and—'

'Wonder why,' Tony interjected.

'It's fine, Diane, really,' Finn said.

'OK, good.' She nodded, just as the hotline clanged, echoing all through the vehicle bay.

During the day, emergency calls from the central dispatcher were picked up by the receptionist and crews were paged, either over the loudspeaker or on their personal pagers. After hours, the phone was everyone's responsibility, and there were two distinct rings, the loud 'hotline', which indicated a call-out, or the normal ring, dubbed 'friendly fire' by the ambulance officers.

The latter could mean a personal call or some non-urgent administrative matter. It didn't take long to realise which ring was which, and this insistent sound pealing out right now *wasn't* 'friendly fire'.

'We're first cab off the rank,' Diane told Finn, and picked up the phone in the small office which adjoined the vehicle bay.

They left half a minute later, to a reported road traffic accident some distance out of town. Since RTAs were an automatic priority one, Diane hit the lights and sirens as soon as they were through the doors.

So much for seeing Anna. Finn had barely got a chance to say a quick, 'Hello.'

'Bloody idiot. Come on, I do have my indicators *on*. Could you get out of my lane, you stupid great galoot. Lady, let's not *cause* an accident here! Oh…' Diane descended into a string of colourful oaths which she would have been horrified to hear her children use, punctuated by a quick 'Sorry, Finn,' before she lowered the volume and muttered some more impatient suggestions to her fellow road-users.

Finn just shut it all out, turned to the window and thought about Anna as they veered round two corners in quick succession and gained the highway, heading west.

He had never felt like this about a woman before, not even at the height of the best affairs he'd ever had. And 'affairs' was the right word, he could now see. At the time he'd dutifully called them 'relationships,' taken them seriously, and a couple of them he'd really tried to make work.

He'd met two sets of parents over the years. For ten months, a few years back, he'd tried extremely hard for Trudy's sake to get interested in the grooming and showing of a certain breed of miniature dog, about which Trudy had been passionate. Some people might have said she was obsessive, in fact, far more so than any of the other very pleasant dog enthusiasts he had met through her, and in the end he just hadn't been able to stand it. Sorry, but did a dog really need that many kinds of grooming brush?

For a far briefer time before that he had been engaged, but before the half-carat diamond solitaire ring had even been paid for, Simone had started thumbing through a truly enormous stack of bride magazines, talking about engraved swizzle sticks and professional calligraphy on the 250 invitations.

That had been scary enough, but when she had, with excruciating tact, suggested that Finn take a course in etiquette for businessmen, and had confessed that she hoped he'd soon join her father's extremely successful appliance manufacturing enterprise as a junior executive... Well, it really had been a very short engagement!

Anna was different. So different!

He wasn't at all sure that he could put it into words, but it was like...oh, like tasting thick King Island cream on a hot peach pie, after you'd been fobbed off for years with insipid trickles of milk pumped up with gelatine. Or like that glorious wind-swept beach the other day, after half a lifetime of paddling in artificial ponds.

It wasn't just physical. He knew about physical. Physical was what made a man put up with entire, stress-filled, detail-obsessed weekends dedicated to two over-pampered, snappy little pedigreed dogs, when he much preferred mongrels with happily muddied paws. Physical was what had made him briefly consider trying to masquerade as something he wasn't—i.e. born with a silver spoon in his mouth—because if a woman looked as gorgeous as Simone did, then she'd eventually lose that stiffness and repugnance when he tried to kiss her, wouldn't she?

A lot of men were like that, he knew, particularly when they were still wet behind the ears. If they liked the packaging enough, they tricked themselves into thinking they liked its contents as well. The unlucky ones never realised their mistake.

Oh, Lord, I feel so damned lucky today!

Finn knew it wasn't just the packaging with Anna. They shared so much. Their difficult backgrounds, which didn't necessarily matter. Their criteria for what made a satisfying career, which mattered more. Their relaxed approach to leisure time, which was absolutely crucial.

And their physical response to each other...the way his every sense had been awakened by her, the way they set each other aflame, melted together, sparked fireworks... Well, that was the rich, thick, gooey, flavour-filled icing on a very well-made cake.

CHAPTER SEVEN

'CHECK the map for me, can you, Finn?' Diane said.

'Yep.'

'What were the details again?'

'Intersection of Route B51 and Route C735.'

'Should be coming up, right?'

'Yeah…' He looked at the map and at the odometer. 'Another two or three k's.'

He had already filled in the initial details on the patient care report. Priority number. Time received. Time of departure. Location. There were still a lot of blank spaces left, and if this turned out to be a major emergency, the rest of the details might have to wait their turn.

The possibility of this being the case increased as further details came in from Cathy, who was on dispatch tonight. The police were already on scene, and had relayed information about what they had found.

Single occupant, injured and trapped inside the vehicle.

Diane was slowing, and they could both see the site of the accident now. Finn could have judged just from the state of the vehicle that their skills would be needed, even without Cathy's radioed update.

The car's driver, probably either drunk, tired or distracted, possibly as the result of a mechanical problem with the vehicle, had lost control on a bend and had hit a tree at some speed. A passing motorist had called in the accident on his mobile phone, then had disappeared before the police had been able to talk to him, claiming 'an important appointment'.

The police car's blue lights were flashing, and as Diane drew to a halt Finn could hear more sirens behind him. It would be the road rescue crew from their own service.

Luck.

Finn had reflected just a short while earlier on his own feeling of luckiness today. He shared it with the female patient he and Diane delivered to Teymouth Hospital an hour later. Distraction had turned out to be the culprit, not drunkenness, fatigue or mechanical failure.

Lesley Palmer, aged thirty-two, was afraid of spiders, and a very large and very hairy—though harmless—specimen of the huntsman variety had somehow infiltrated the car and crawled across the inside of the windscreen just a half metre from her terrified gaze. She had remained in control enough to slow down, but when it had crawled rapidly around to the door and disappeared somewhere near her thigh, she'd panicked, missed the left-curving bend and crumpled the right side of the vehicle against a tree.

Only the fact that she'd already lost considerable speed had kept her alive and in good shape. There was evidence of mild concussion, a lacerated shoulder and a broken right leg.

Lesley's first words to the police, and then to Finn, Diane and the rescue crew were, 'Can you see the spider? Where's it gone?' She remained almost more shaken about her close encounter with eight hairy legs than about the accident itself.

Finn and Diane satisfied themselves that her airway, breathing and circulation were secure and that her head injury wasn't dangerous, put in an intravenous line containing morphine for pain, and splinted her leg before sliding the stretcher into the ambulance. It clunked into place like a freight car shunting into a siding, and Lesley said again, 'It didn't come in here, did it? Could you check before we drive off?'

'The spider?'

'Yes, please!' Her teeth were chattering, and Finn had already taken precautions to maintain her body temperature. She was covered in a blanket, and the small fan heater in the back of the ambulance was warming the air.

'You're really scared of them, aren't you?' he said.

'Phobic,' Lesley agreed. 'They're such a hideous combination of hairiness and unpredictability.'

'Like a lot of men.'

She tried to laugh, but her jaw just chattered mercilessly. Her limbs were shaking, too.

'There are courses you can take to overcome various phobias,' Finn offered.

But Lesley shuddered. 'Do you think I want *not* to be scared? The very thought…'

He made a note on the form under 'History of Previous Problems'. 'Patient's arachnophobia was life-threatening on this occasion and could be again. Follow-up should steer towards therapy, if patient can be persuaded.'

There was plenty of time to fill in the rest of the form as well, since Lesley had soon calmed down considerably. The morphine was acting as a sedative as well as containing the pain from her fractured leg. The hand-over at Teymouth's Casualty entrance was uneventful, with some grimaces and raised eyebrows about the spider, and Finn and Diane were back at headquarters just before nine o'clock.

Diane hadn't sworn once on the final leg of the journey, but said in a rather uneasy voice, 'I'm not all that keen on large, hairy spiders myself.'

'Would you panic in the same situation?'

'No, I'd do my usual and swear my bloody head off!'

Anna turned out to be scared of spiders, too. She was sitting at the table in the staffroom with her crewing partner, Ron, and an off-duty paramedic, Dave Thorburn. The latter had dropped in to report a win for the night-time touch football team in which several of the paramedics played. He was also trying to arrange a roster swap with Anna, but without much success.

Finn hid a grin at this. He knew...*hoped* he knew...why she didn't want to change. She was rostered with him again more than once over the next few weeks, before she returned to flight crewing.

He sat down next to her, deliberately brushing her thigh with his own beneath the table as Diane raised the spider question once more.

'Makes you think,' she said.

'Wouldn't worry me at all,' Dave claimed. 'I could have one crawling all over my hand and I wouldn't raise a sweat.'

Ron admitted to an initial jump of the heart when he'd had a similar experience a year or two earlier, while Anna said, 'I'd do a Diane and scare the thing back.' Everyone laughed.

Ah, this was nice, Finn thought. Much nicer than last week. Then he'd only imagined how it would feel to kiss her. Now he knew, and he could tell she was thinking of it, too. Their eyes met when she got up from the table briefly to make tea. Her thigh was returning the pressure of his. It was a secret they shared, although a part of him wanted to shout it to the world.

The interlude didn't last. She and Ron were called out to a patient with chest pain, Dave left and Diane settled in front of the television with some knitting. She loved her American police dramas on a Monday night. For Finn, some of the images reminded him too closely of a bad day at work. He prowled around, ate some supper and almost wasn't sorry when the hotline cut across the quiet night-time atmosphere.

This time, two ambulances were required, and he knew he'd see Anna when they got there. Not that he'd have wished it on her, because it turned out to be an ugly scene…could have come straight out of the police show he'd just avoided.

There had been a fight outside a pub, and two people were injured. There was still a crew of uneasy, half-plastered men and a couple of women hanging around, with only one or two of them having a clue about what to do. Anna and Ron were already at work over the most seriously injured patient, while the police had just arrived as well and were asking questions, to which they were getting sullen, unwilling responses.

The second patient, Finn and Diane's responsibility, had been propped up against a wall with a makeshift wad of jackets and sweaters to cushion him. He was bleeding from a wound on his temple, had several angry red bruises and was holding two teeth and a mouthful of blood in a handkerchief in the palm of his hand. Diane crouched beside him, ordered everyone to clear away and began to ask him some questions.

'He's lost consciousness,' Anna reported urgently to Finn about her patient. He was beside Diane, and Anna had come straight over, looking for another opinion to confirm her sense of what was going on. There was a young policeman hovering, too.

'He was groggy when we got here,' she went on. 'We talked to him and got a couple of details. He knew his name. But now he's slipping deeper, so we're going to make tracks as fast as we can.'

'I don't like the sound of that.'

'No, I know,' she agreed. 'But isn't it just wasting time to stabilise him here?'

'Can you intubate a patient in a moving vehicle?'

'Intubate?' she echoed blankly. 'I don't intubate at all. It's against protocol.'

'Hell, that's right! Vern said it's still a controversial area down here. He's expecting that will change, right?'

'That's why we carry the equipment. He'd like it to change.'

'But I guess it hasn't yet.'

'Anna, let's go,' Ron said with a snap in his voice. 'His breathing sounds bad. Very bad. I'm going to put in an airway and set him up with a mask. Let's get him in the back.'

But even as he said it, the patient's breathing was deteriorating further, to a low, irregular and laboured gurgle.

'That's not going to be enough,' Finn said. 'You'll lose him before you get there.'

'We have to try,' Ron argued. 'Unless you've got something else to suggest?'

They were all talking in rapid mumbles. The crowd around the scene was thinning, but several people still stood by, and the police presence had coloured their mood. This was serious now, and charges would be laid. Two women were crying, and there was a young man raving on incoherently as his friends attempted to calm him.

'I'll intubate,' Finn answered. 'Or you'll lose him.

You will! Listen to that! He's going deeper every second.'

'On your head, mate,' Ron pointed out accurately.

'I'll take the risk. Let's move him into the car. I don't need this lot as an audience.'

'Diane, what have you got?' Ron turned to her as she talked to the other patient.

'Needs hospital treatment, but not critical. I'll get him in the back and clean him up a bit, Finn.'

'Police want to talk to him at some point,' Anna came in.

'If you want to intubate, Finn,' Diane went on, 'if you feel confident, then do it. I agree it's that or arrive at the hospital with…'

A deceased patient. None of them said it, but they all understood. They had the training to recognise the signs of progressively deepening unconsciousness, and it was happening fast.

Anna and Ron got out their stretcher and moved the patient onto it, then slid it efficiently into the back of their vehicle, where it clicked into place. Finn had already climbed inside to get out the equipment he needed from the respiratory kit. He had the oxygen supply ready, as well as tubing and tape, by the time the patient was inside.

It wasn't a difficult job. Took practice, and you had to know what to feel and listen for. Measure the length of tubing, tape it at the mouth, check that it had gone down the right pipe. No good having it lead into the stomach. Finn usually managed to get it right first time, and tonight was no exception. It felt good when he set the respirator going and heard the regular rhythm start, instead of the dangerously erratic and laboured sounds of a moment ago.

This wasn't the end of the road for this patient, of course, but it was the vital first step. If you couldn't keep them breathing, nothing else mattered. His heart rate was acceptable at least. Blood pressure low but livable. No fractures other than that skull. Several facial bruises, like his sparring partner.

Would the injury to the brain resolve, or leave a lasting legacy? As usual, Finn himself might never know. Although on this occasion, he amended, when there might be professional repercussions, he might know the outcome in every detail.

'OK,' he said to Anna and Ron, 'he's yours again. Might see you there.'

He jumped out of the back of the car and went to help Diane, who was having a hard time persuading the other injured party that he needed a ride. Anna started up her lights and sirens and car 118 disappeared off into the night.

'I feel fine,' Diane's patient was insisting expansively, a night of drinking still colouring his perception. 'Just needed to catch my breath. Thanks for mopping up my face.'

'It's still bleeding, Joe,' Diane told him. 'It needs stitches.'

'Can't you do that?'

'Not our job, mate,' Finn came in. 'Let's go, shall we?'

'What about my mates? We were celebrating, till that idiot came and insulted my girlfriend.'

'Leave your mates, Joe,' Finn said. 'But if there's one of them who hasn't been drinking...'

'We had Geoff as designated driver.'

'He can bring your girlfriend, then, to hold your hand when you get there.'

'All right.' Joe shrugged. He only looked about nineteen. 'Guess I'll go, then. That other idiot, is he going to be all right? Didn't hit him that hard, but he went down weird against the wall.'

'You're going to have to tell all that to the police.' Finn didn't point out how serious the issue might become if Anna and Ron's patient sustained permanent brain damage or, worse, if he didn't survive.

'The police? Yeah, I guess,' the man said vaguely, as if noticing their uniformed presence for the first time. 'That's awkward, isn't it?'

'One way of putting it,' Finn agreed.

They met up with Anna and Ron again in the ambulance entrance at the hospital. Their patient had been raced off to surgery, with the expectation that there was a build-up of pressure in the brain which would need to be relieved at once. After he and Diane had handed over their own patient to the accident and emergency staff, Finn saw that Anna and Ron hadn't left yet, though they'd pulled their vehicle ahead so that they weren't blocking the bay.

'Feeling OK about that?' Ron wanted to know, approaching Finn.

Anna didn't speak, but her eyes did it for her. She was even more interested in Finn's answer than Ron was.

'Don't know,' Finn said. 'Did what felt right, I know that. Pretty confident he wouldn't have made it otherwise. I mean, we all were, weren't we? I'll let you know what sort of a reaction I get from higher up. You think it'll be bad?'

'I'd say it completely depends on the outcome for the patient, if you want the truth, Finn,' Ron answered bluntly. 'You could be in deep...uh, shampoo, let's call it. He's young, and he's probably got parents, who are about to get the worst news of their lives, and—' He stopped and shrugged.

'Well, at least they still have a bedside to come to, and a warm hand to hold,' Finn pointed out. He didn't plan to spend the next few days regretting the fact that he'd saved a man's life.

Seeing Anna's wide, worried eyes still on him, he was sure he'd done the right thing, and he'd rather spend his spare moments thinking about her. Oh, yes! Thinking about her in enormous and very pleasurable detail.

Something was trying to drag Anna out of sleep. Her subconscious fought it, tried to incorporate it into a dream, but finally she realised what it was.

The phone, ringing insistently.

Her first thought was that it had to be Finn, but when she looked at the clock and saw it was two in the afternoon she was less sure. Would he call her at this time of the day when they were both in the middle of two night shifts? Unlikely for a fellow paramedic to make that mistake unless it was urgent.

The continuing ring suggested that it might be, and she stumbled crookedly from the bed, through the doorway and lunged for the instrument, parked on the coffee-table.

'Hi, Anna!'

'Kendra?'

'Yeah, is this a bad time? You sound—'

'I had a night shift.'

'Oh, so-o-rry!' Kendra moaned. 'I woke you up! Shall I hang up?'

'It's all right. I'm awake now. It's fine,' Anna answered her, perhaps a little too impatiently.

Guilty conscience?

Kendra was carrying Finn's child. That was staking your claim on a man in no uncertain terms. And yet when Anna and Finn were together it just didn't feel like that. The painful caving sensation in the pit of Anna's stomach told her that she had to face up to a harsh truth, however. The good, easy feeling about her love for Finn was wrong. There were issues to be dealt with. Issues she'd had an inkling of from the beginning, which meant it was high time she tackled them head on.

'How are you, Kendra?' she asked cautiously.

'Oh, revolting. That's why I'm ringing.'

'I can't do much for you at this distance.' Anna laughed awkwardly. 'You should see your doctor.'

'No, not that kind of revolting. Well, partly. I'm getting so big. Just feeling a bit down, that's all. No one to talk to. Mum's driving me crazy. Says *she* never put on that much weight, and *she* never had food cravings and *she* would never have got herself into my situation anyway. Trouble is…' she laughed '…I'm such an easy target. It's all true!'

Kendra gave another laugh that was more like a sob, and there was a long, snuffly silence at the far end of the phone.

'Ah, Kendra,' Anna soothed.

Suddenly she was miserable. At heart, she cared a lot about Kendra. They were very different, but they had always been allies, plotting their escape from Fryerstown in their teens. Life was an upside-down sort of thing sometimes. Kendra was the one who had planned on nursing as a career, but that hadn't been creative enough for her. Anna had seen herself as an artist, yet had ended up in a profession that was closely allied to nursing.

'Have a good cry and you'll feel better,' she said in-adequately. 'I wish I was there to help.'

The words weren't even out of her mouth before she knew what she had to do. 'In fact,' she added, 'Come and stay, Kendra. You turned me down before, I know, but think about it again, please! It'd be…well, good for you, and…you know. I'd love to see you. Molly-coddle you a bit. Sounds like you need it.'

'Oh, Anna, I don't know if—'

'Please, Kendra. You could even have the baby here. Teymouth has a good hospital, you know that. I have a sofa-bed in the lounge-room. With my hours we'd get to spend time together, but you'd still have privacy when I'm at work, particularly on nights.'

'I've got no money.'

'Don't worry about that. I'll take care of the bus ticket. Or you could even fly…'

Kendra raised several more objections, but from her changing tone Anna could hear the idea catching hold in her mind, like flame beginning to lick around the edges of paper.

Aware that she wasn't offering even a hint of the most compelling reason for Kendra to come to Teymouth—to settle things with Finn—Anna held her breath in hope, and was rewarded with, 'I'll think about it. I'll ring you again in a couple of days, OK?'

'OK, Kendra. But take it seriously, won't you?'

When she had put down the phone, Anna felt churned up to the point of nausea. She had to go and lean over the kitchen sink and take some deep breaths, then pour herself a large glass of water and drink it very slowly.

She knew she had done the right thing, but it hadn't been easy. There was still a nagging temptation inside her to hope like crazy that Kendra would decide not to come. Or at least not until after the baby was born, by which time she and Finn would have cemented their relationship into something strong and unbreakable and—

No. *No!* You couldn't build something strong if it had no foundations, and a relationship between herself and Finn as things stood would be a relationship built on quicksand. Finn had to know about Kendra's baby. Anna didn't know what a difference it would make to him—to his plans and goals, to how he felt about herself, to his feelings for Kendra.

But it wasn't her place to second-guess any of that. In fact, she only had one simple task right now, and that was to step aside, take herself out of the equation so that Finn and Kendra could resolve things on their own.

And I may never be able to step back in! she knew. It might already be over before it's even truly begun.

'Not hanging out with us tonight?' Finn said to Anna that evening, after various dinners had disappeared into various hungry mouths.

There had only been one call-out so far, an elderly woman taken to hospital after a fall.

'Not tonight,' Anna said, trying to make it light. 'Too tired! I'm going to snooze in front of telly.'

'Didn't sleep today? Bad girl!' he teased.

There was a little light of curiosity and uncertainty in his eyes, which Anna could read very clearly and didn't blame him for. She knew she was sending out strange signals, in contrast to the private but unmistakable heat of the past couple of days. They could read each other so clearly. He wasn't certain that something was wrong, but he was wary all the same. She wondered, too, if last night's lifesaving breach of protocol was on his mind.

They hadn't heard anything about the outcome of that yet, but at some point they would.

She took a deep breath and said deliberately, 'My cousin Kendra phoned at two o'clock, right in the middle of my sleep, and I couldn't fall back afterwards.'

'Kendra?' he said in surprise, picking up at once on the unusual name. 'Not Kendra Phillips?'

'Yes.' She nodded, refusing to feign any surprise. 'You know her from Melbourne, don't you?'

'Knew,' he corrected quickly, frowning. 'I wouldn't say "know". I haven't seen her for months. I had no idea you two were cousins.'

'There's no reason why you should have,' she told him.

'Then how did you know that I knew her?'

'She mentioned you once or twice.'

'Right…'

He raised his eyebrows briefly, then clicked his tongue before turning to nod affirmatively to Diane's offer of coffee. Anna could see he was trying to dismiss the apparently unimportant exchange, but that he couldn't quite do it. It set her even further on edge than she already was…and that was saying something!

She was so tempted to tell him the truth. *I know you had a fling with Kendra. She's pregnant with your child. She still wants you, but she's waiting until the baby is born because she doesn't trust you to care when she's so big and bloated, with bad skin, and when the baby is just a cloud of imminent burden on the horizon.*

I trust you to care. I know if there's anything still possible between you and Kendra it wouldn't make a scrap of difference to you how she looks and how much of a responsibility the baby would be, but she…doesn't know you as well as I do, I guess, and she doesn't have that faith.

But she had already decided that it wouldn't be fair of her to say any of this. She had no right. Telling him had to remain Kendra's prerogative, and her choice. Anna could exercise her powers of persuasion over her cousin, but couldn't take matters into her own hands.

She was under no illusions about how painful it was going to be. If Kendra didn't ring again by Thursday, Friday at the latest…

She did, however, on Wednesday at one-thirty in the afternoon, when Anna had had even less sleep than the day before.

'Oh, no, did I wake you *again*?'

'It really isn't a good time to phone, Kendra,' Anna said wearily. 'Anyone who works night shifts will tell you that.'

Most people took a while to wind down after they came off duty at seven-thirty. They would run errands and have something to eat, then subside into a sleep that was almost like being drugged at around lunchtime.

'But it doesn't matter,' she went on. 'Just tell me what you've decided.'

'I'm coming down.'

'Great! When?' The sooner, the better.

'The Tuesday after next. I have a pre-natal on the Friday, and then some friends will be in town over the weekend. I'll get the bus on Tuesday morning.'

'I could arrange a pre-natal appointment here,' Anna offered.

'Well, no, I really want to see Rob and Linda. You don't have to worry about me. I mean, I really, *really* want to come. Talking to you made a huge difference yesterday. But now that I know I have, like, an escape valve, I'd rather wait.'

She talked on for several more minutes, asked about Anna's life and made her laugh once or twice with a deliberately exaggerated account of her pregnancy trials and tribulations, then rang off.

Anna then had to sit on the bed and mutter aloud, 'Heaven help me, I had no idea I was such a brilliant actress!' She'd somehow managed to hide just how excruciating the prospect was of almost two weeks of waiting for even the hope of a resolution, especially since she was expected to go to dinner at Finn's on Friday night.

CHAPTER EIGHT

ANNA would have cancelled dinner if she'd had any reason to believe that Finn would have let her do it without a fight. But she knew he wouldn't.

He still had that same light in his eyes when he met her in the doorway of his little farm cottage on Friday night at eight. It contained a mixture of apprehension, uncertainty, anger, desire and sheer fight that flickered back and forth like a candle flame in a brisk breeze.

'You found the place a'right, then?' he said.

'I drive an ambulance, remember? We're trained to make sense of garbled directions.'

'Which mine weren't.'

'Exactly. So of course I found it all right. It's a great spot, Finn, and a great little place.'

'I like it,' he agreed. 'I didn't want something in town. Never lived on a farm before, though.'

'Ah, the smell of the pigs, the sound of the roosters crowing at dawn,' she teased.

'Love it,' he agreed, and he was ninety per cent serious.

'Seems a piece of luck that this place was for rent. It's the old farmhouse, right?'

'Right. The farm people now live in that well-maintained but pretty characterless new place at the top of the hill. They rented this house out to tourists for a few years, but they're getting old now, and felt a steady tenant would be less work, if not as lucrative.'

'As I said, lucky for you.'

'Have a good look,' he invited.

'If you don't mind.'

'Well…hope you'll soon feel right at home here, so of course I don't mind,' he said lightly.

Anna ignored the opening he was offering her. They hadn't touched, yet, which was her fault. Without making it obvious, she'd sidestepped his relaxed attempts to get near her. She had slipped past him to put the bottle of wine she'd brought on the dining table, and now she was diligently going over the house, taking inventory of the old-fashioned fireplace, the modernised bathroom, the two neatly furnished bedrooms.

It wasn't easy. She would have loved to fold herself into his arms, and knew exactly how good it would feel.

But conversation and curiosity seemed like the best ways to distance herself, so she kept them up relentlessly. Peering out of the kitchen window to the view of poppy fields slanted with late golden sunlight, she asked, 'Planning to stay here long?'

'I'm saving to buy a place eventually. Preferably with a little bit of land. I should be ready to start looking in a few months, but I wanted to settle into the work first, take my time with it. How about you? Do you feel as if you're in Teymouth for good?'

'I'm happy here,' she hedged. 'And it's the only place in Tasmania where I can use my flight training.'

'Not the helicopter service out of Hobart?'

'Hate helicopters!' She shuddered. 'I tried going up in one a couple of times to see if I'd like it, but I get motion sickness the way I never have in a plane.'

Finn poured some wine, checked the chicken that was roasting in the oven and they waded through another half-hour of this sort of conversation while they waited to eat.

Well, 'waded' was the wrong word. It was nice. Pleasant. They learned things about each other—factual details, past history, a few more tastes and preferences—but it wasn't the sort of conversation they should have been having, and they both knew it.

The simple roast chicken he'd stuffed with two whole lemons was delicious. Anna complimented him on it as they cleared away, and was about to launch into some trivial and relentlessly upbeat question about what other hidden domestic talents he possessed.

Before she could frame the words, however, he turned to her with a pained, intense expression on his face and asked quietly, 'How much longer are you going to put us both through this torture, Anna?'

'I didn't—'

'Yes, you did.' He reached out, took Anna by the waist with both hands and pulled her against him with one fluid, magnetic motion.

'You've been doing it quite deliberately. I went along with it because—hell, because I don't rush a woman if she doesn't want to be rushed, but it's more than that, isn't it? What's wrong? *What's wrong?*' he repeated softly and urgently. 'Didn't we get over the problem you thought you had about me when we first met? That seemed to disappear for a while, but now it's back. Or maybe it's something different, but it matters just as much. Or even more.'

He had her right up against him, length to length, and he was tracing the line and shape of her lips with his fingertips, back and forth, as he spoke. He was frowning, exploring her lips, watching them gradually part as if it was the most hypnotic sight in the world.

The kitchen where they stood was silent except for the guttural tick of an ancient electric clock, and Anna could hardly breathe. Her heart ached. Chest pain. Priority one call-out. Ha ha. There was no medicine you could give for *this* ache. Not yet. Everything she felt, every explanation she wanted to give, had to hang fire until Kendra arrived, eleven days from now, and the prospect of waiting, and of keeping silent, seemed intolerable.

'Don't ask me about it, Finn,' she croaked at last. 'Please!'

Weakly, she tilted her face forward and just…sort of…leaned her forehead against his mouth, knowing she was inviting a kiss…a very long kiss…but unable to stop herself.

He took it incredibly slowly, as if giving her chance after chance to change her mind. First there was that firm mouth, imprinting itself on her forehead over and over, then the fingers of one hand, scooping and stroking along her jaw, lifting her face once more so that his lips could trail down across her closed lids, past her cheekbones and the side of her nose to her mouth—oh, yes, her mouth—where they rested, played, supped.

'Why can't I ask you about it?' he demanded at last, his own voice croaking now, and his mouth hardly taking the trouble to lift from hers.

'Because it's not something I—' She broke off.

How could she even begin to explain the reason for this barrier between them without usurping Kendra's right to tell Finn about the baby?

'Oh, this is hopeless!' she exclaimed, and turned herself abruptly out of his arms. 'Do you think I want to be going through this? Do you think I want it to be this hard?'

Wild questions, blurted without stopping for thought. They were unfair.

'Thanks for clarifying the situation,' Finn said, the bite of his sarcasm tightening up his face.

'I told you, Finn, I—'

'You've told me absolutely nothing.'

'I know. That's the whole point. I can't. I'm sorry. I know I'm not making any sense. I should go.'

'Should you? Wouldn't it be better if we tried to communicate a little better? I'm not a quitter, Anna, and when I have a strong vision about possibilities, about the future—'

'I can't,' she repeated.

She was fighting her own will as much as she was fighting him. She knew how close she was to giving in to him. Wouldn't it be easy...perfect...just to snuggle into his arms and confess everything?

You're going to share a baby with my cousin, but you don't care about her, do you? You care about me.

If she said that, here, now, she would win this. She was almost sure of it. But if she did that, she would be aware for ever afterwards of the layer of poison lying against the bedrock of their relationship, like the poisoned layers of soil around the copper mine in Fryerstown.

'I'm going home, Finn. Thanks for dinner. I mean that.' She blinked back tears. 'But I don't think we ought to see each other for a while. Let things settle.'

'Not see each other? We're rostered together for two shifts next week and another two the week after that.'

'You know what I mean. We can keep it separate, can't we?'

'Can we?'

'We'll have to.'

Finn nodded briefly. Anna knew he wasn't giving up—*hoped* he wasn't, heaven help her—and wondered frantically, Do I trust myself? I've got eleven days left to ruin this totally before Kendra gets here.

They stumbled through another minute or two of awkward phrases, then she gained the relative safety and peace of her small car and went home to a sleepless night, wishing she'd cancelled the evening with him and not gone to his place at all.

'I'm obliged to convey to you in fairly strong terms that you went against protocol by intubating that patient, Finn,' Vern Land said, facing Finn across the large desk in his private office.

'I'm aware of that, but the patient survived, and I understand he's looking set to make a full recovery,' Finn pointed out.

'So I hear. Congratulations. It's always a good feeling, isn't it?'

'I'm getting mixed signals here, Vern.'

'I'm giving out mixed signals here, Finn,' the older man parodied deliberately. There was a twinkle in his dark eyes, and a crooked little twist of ironic amusement at the corner of his mouth, both of which belied the formality of his uniform and his tidy desk.

'You know the situation we're in,' he went on. 'But just in case it's unclear, I'll say it again. There's a move to change the protocols of the service regarding the intubation of patients by our paramedics. One of the reasons I recruited you was because I knew you were well versed in the technique and took care to keep your experience current.'

'Spent a day in the operating theatre just before I left Melbourne, keeping my hand in,' Finn confirmed.

'It's a mechanical skill,' Vern agreed. 'Gets better with practice. But, yes, I'm patting you on the back with one hand and slapping your wrist with the other. I'd like to see the protocol officially changed, but until it does I have to remind you that, had there been a poor outcome for the patient concerned, and had the patient's family chosen to pursue the issue, your failure to adhere to protocol would have left you without the official umbrella of the service's protection.'

'I take your point,' Finn said. 'I knew it at the time, and I should stress that Ron, Anna and Diane all reminded me about the fact. It was my decision to go ahead and, to be honest, in the heat of the moment the immediate survival of the patient was the only thing I wanted to consider. But, yes,' he repeated, 'I do take your point.'

'Good,' Vern said, 'because it's not one I enjoy having to repeat. We all have to go through the motions sometimes.'

A few minutes later, Finn left Vern's office, knowing he'd been let off rather lightly. He and Vern had both spoken of 'mixed signals'. It seemed to be the story of his life at the moment, both professionally and personally, and he was in no doubt that it was the personal signals which were the biggest headache.

He'd worked day shifts on Saturday and Sunday, and had had Monday, Tuesday and Wednesday off. Now it was Thursday, a warm February morning, and he was rostered to crew with Anna both today and tomorrow. The way he felt about this fact, it seemed impossible that they'd only known each other a month.

The day started off uneventfully, with the usual checking and cleaning of their vehicle. Finn liked the steadier energy of a day shift after the high drama of night-time call-outs and low ebb of fitful sleep in the stand-down rooms. There were more people about during the day.

The crews driving non-urgent patient transport vehicles came and went. The office staff had queries about leave application forms and pay-slips. Sometimes there were training sessions in progress in the conference room.

Unfortunately, none of it was enough to distract him from the fact that he and Anna were paired together. It was too hot for overalls, so they both wore their navy pants and short-sleeved shirts, and Anna probably wouldn't have liked it if she'd known how his gaze kept getting caught by the faintest outline of a pale blue bra beneath the crisp white.

Or would she? he wondered, helplessly angry, helplessly ready to forgive. Maybe she'd like it a lot.

This chemistry in the air wasn't just emanating from him. Her whole body changed when he came within touching range. Brushing past her to check the oxygen kit, he both saw and felt the little shudder of need and awareness she gave. He watched her deliberately with his peripheral vision and saw an unmistakable softening in her limbs and a new light in her face.

He almost, *almost* reached out to snatch a kiss by pulling her head towards his, but at the last minute the tingle of anger replaced the sizzle of desire and he pushed the hot physical need back down into his gut and let it go.

What are you doing to me, Anna Brewster? What are you doing to both of us?

They started the day with a P1 call-out. As so often happened, it was 'chest pain', and didn't look like a false alarm on this occasion. The patient was an elderly man, grey and scared and in pain, and his wife was darting about like a tame park pigeon, flappy and annoying and relentless.

She kept giving them details they didn't need, and

didn't stop talking long enough for them to ask questions about the details that they *did* need, and both he and Anna had to battle to do their job efficiently.

He knew the wife couldn't help her reaction. She was plain, damn terrified, and some people reacted to fear that way, but it was a relief when her daughter arrived to drive her to the hospital in the wake of the ambulance, and a bigger relief once they were on their way, with Finn at the wheel and Anna tackling things cheerfully in the back.

They had only just arrived back at headquarters when they were dispatched again. This time, it was an elderly Alzheimer's patient, aged ninety-one, who had wandered away from his home and fallen in the street. He was extremely suspicious of the young man who had found him and called the ambulance on a mobile phone, and then he didn't recognise his daughter-in-law. She had spent the past fifteen minutes frantically driving around the neighbourhood in search of him, and was in a state.

Although his physical injuries didn't appear very serious, Finn and Anna decided to bring him to hospital just to make sure. He seemed too agitated for his daughter-in-law to handle on her own, and in the ambulance, with Anna driving this time, he was convinced for most of the journey that he was being kidnapped.

Although he had settled down and regained some lucidity by the time they reached the hospital, it was distressing for everyone involved, and Finn and Anna were both in need of a break when they headed back to headquarters once more. Typically, they didn't get one, and were diverted to another P1 call-out before they'd even got halfway back.

'Caller very agitated,' reported Cathy Tyndale, who was on dispatch today. 'Patient is a three-year-old boy pulled from the family pool and they can't revive him. Caller is the patient's mother. There's also a neighbour present, and I'm relaying instructions.'

Anna activated the lights and sirens and tightened her grip on the wheel, while Finn responded to the dispatcher. It was an address in West Teymouth, near where Anna lived, and they were only a few minutes away.

But when they arrived, the little boy was still unresponsive and, after giving it everything they had, on the spot, for fifteen minutes—for most of them Finn knew it was beyond hope—they gave up, and just had to take the little body away. Death would be pronounced officially by a doctor at the hospital.

'Where was the mother?' Anna asked, breaking a long silence, as they neared headquarters once more.

'On the phone,' Finn answered, then summarised tersely, 'His ball went over the pool fence. She didn't realise he was strong enough to drag an outdoor chair over and climb on it to reach the child-lock on the pool gate. The ball was in the pool when they found him. He must have been stretching out for it and lost his balance.'

Anna nodded but didn't speak. She had been too involved in attempting to resuscitate the boy to take in the ragged explanations of the mother and the neighbour, and Finn understood that now she needed to know. It would all go down on the report form as well.

They both felt terrible. Fate didn't always give you the opportunity to pull out a miracle, the way he had with the young man he'd intubated outside the pub ten days ago. In this case, they knew, it had been too late from the moment the little boy had been lifted from the pool.

There was another silence, until headquarters loomed

into view. Finn took the opportunity to say gruffly, 'Are you going to be all right?'

'Yes,' Anna answered. 'But, oh, it *burns*, doesn't it?'

'I know, like a big, hot rock in your stomach,' Finn agreed.

'Makes me want to take out a full page ad in the newspaper or something, saying "Parents, don't trust pools. Don't trust fenced pools. Don't trust locked gates. Teach your kids to swim and, still, *never* take your eye off them when there's a pool." That poor mother…'

'Shake it off, Anna.'

'Why, will *you*?'

'No, not for a while,' he admitted.

What he didn't admit to was the effect it had on him in regard to Anna. How it made him want to hold her. Not say anything. No more words of wisdom and comfort. Just hold her and talk carefully about other things, because a reality in this job was that you had to see people die. Kids sometimes.

They had a late, quiet lunch together in the staffroom, reporting the difficult details of their morning to another crew and getting nods of sympathy and understanding. Then the place began to empty out. Another crew went to a peak-hour RTA which turned out to be minor, and it looked as if the drama of this shift might be over.

Nope. Not yet.

Another urgent call-out, at six-fifteen. They were due to finish at seven. Finn was at the wheel this time, and they arrived at a modest little house in the suburb of Garside to find their patient, Jill Haley, deep in the throes of transitional labour. A taxi had just pulled up outside, Jill's husband had screeched to a halt in the driveway, and two young children were clinging to their poor mother, quite unable to understand why their cuddling and comforting weren't wanted. Under the griller, sausages were burning.

'Think you can make it to the hospital?' Finn asked. 'Or should we try and do it here?'

'Here?' Jill Haley thew up her hands in horror, then stormed raggedly at her husband to deal with the sausages and the children *now*, and not waste time trying to get her to do her stupid breathing techniques, which hadn't been any help with the last two and certainly wouldn't be any help this time.

In fact, however, as each contraction came with scarcely a pause in between, she was breathing more or less as she should—great, desperate lungfuls of air.

She couldn't walk through the contractions. Anna and Finn had to use the stretcher to get her into the back of the vehicle, and Finn found himself saying to his partner, 'Can you handle it? I'm not convinced she's going to make it as far as the emergency entrance, let alone the delivery suite.'

'I know.' Anna nodded. 'But I can understand why she wants to try. Too chaotic at home. I'll be fine, Finn. I've done it before.'

'I'll drive fast anyway,' he promised.

Not fast enough, though. He was barely out of the driveway when he heard an urgent screech and bellow coming from the back, 'I've got to push.'

This was followed by Anna's voice saying steadily, 'All right, then, Jill. Let's get you into a position that works for you. Do you want us to stop the car?'

'No.'

'Then I think it's going to have to be on your back. Is that OK?'

'It's how I did the others.'

'Keep panting, that's great.'

From the front, as Finn drove, it was like listening to a radio play. Lots of dialogue and hair-raising sound effects, with a lot of work for the imagination. He couldn't give it too much attention, had to focus on the road and on *not* rocketing around corners in case it threw Anna and Jill off balance at a critical moment.

Once more he heard, 'Let's stop the ambulance, Jill.'

This was followed by, 'No, I want to get to the hospital!'

'You're not going to make it.'

'Don't care. Keep going.'

Finn was just about to override the patient's decision—it really would be easier to have the actual delivery occur in a stationary vehicle, with his input as well—when Anna called forward to him, 'Confirming that, Finn. Keep going, please.' Her tone, he realised, wasn't quite natural.

'Everything OK?' he tossed back to her in a breezy sort of a way.

'Everything's fine.'

It wasn't.

He felt the hairs on the back of his neck prickle to attention, and his whole scalp tightened. Everything *wasn't* fine. He called back once more, 'Don't forget you have another pair of trained hands in front here.'

'I've…uh…heard that some of the hands at the hospital aren't bad either,' she said in a joking way.

Yep, everything was a long way from being fine. It was obvious, however, that Anna didn't want to worry Jill, who had begun to strain and push through a contraction, making the side rails of the stretcher rattle as she gripped them in her effort.

Finn essayed another cautious, encoded enquiry to Anna. 'Any particular hands you're thinking of?'

'Older hands,' she called back, and he couldn't think about what the cryptic words might mean, because he was just about to scream through a red light at a large intersection and there was still a fair bit of traffic on the road.

He was sweating now, but made it through to a quieter street and could relax a bit. Three minutes from the hospital. They were expecting him.

In the back, he heard, 'OK, you're doing really well, Jill. I can see the baby and you're nearly there... Fantastic... Great, keep it coming... Keep it— No! Stop! Pant, Jill. Don't push, OK? Just for a minute? Pant. Hold it. Hold it.'

Hell, what was happening? What was she doing?

'This...doesn't...feel...right!' Jill said, then echoed Finn's own thoughts. 'What's happening? What are you doing?'

'It's... All right, it's fine now.' Palpable relief in Anna's tone. 'Go ahead and push again on the next contraction, OK?'

'Ah-h-h!' Jill gave some huge, panting bellows. 'What was that?'

'It's fine,' Anna repeated. 'Keep going now.'

'What *was* it?'

But the inexorable grip of a new contraction meant that Anna didn't have to answer. Jill was bearing down once more, and Anna was coaching, 'All right, easy bit, now. Yes! Fantastic! He's looking great. Contraction ebbing? Take a break. Now, get ready, last push. Last push. Really, really good push, please, Jill. Everything you've got, with this one. Big breath. Now...'

'*Nnnnnhhh!*'

The hospital came into view, a big, cream brick building, whose ambulance entrance Finn could have driven into blindfolded even after just a few weeks on the job. He heard a newborn cry, above the repeated, drained and delighted sound of 'Oh, oh, oh,' coming from Jill's shaking body.

'You have another boy, Jill, and he's gorgeous. He's healthy, he's fine. We did it!'

'And we're here,' Finn announced, slowing to the smoothest halt he could manage.

The hospital staff took over at once. They had a warming unit ready just in case, and began to suction the baby's nose and throat, although he was already breathing, and screaming, beautifully. Jill was able to hold him on her stomach, right there in the entrance, and within a minute both mother and child had been wheeled inside.

A strange quiet descended, broken by Finn, finally voicing his suspicions aloud. 'Anna, was that baby *breech*?'

'Yes.' She nodded, then gusted a large sigh. 'And I did it, Finn. I delivered him, and I didn't panic, and Jill didn't panic.'

'Because you didn't tell her.'

'She knew something was strange.'

'So did I. That's what you meant about older hands.'

'A nice, old-fashioned doctor who'd delivered dozens of breech babies before they started doing routine Caesareans for breech presentations,' she confirmed.

'But you did it.'

'Had no choice. That little guy wasn't prepared to wait. When I saw a little bottom, instead of a head…! That's why I didn't want you to stop, though. In case the baby got stuck halfway and we really needed help.'

'I knew something was up, but I didn't realise exactly

what until you said she had to give it everything she'd got when I knew the baby was already halfway out.'

'Normally, after the head and shoulders they pop out on their own,' she agreed. 'Oh, Finn, I did it! And I was so scared it was going to go wrong. That last bit with the head... But it didn't, and she has a beautiful, healthy boy!'

He didn't think about it, didn't waste any more time, just took her in his arms and gave her a huge hug. It was a hug he'd have given her even if she'd been Diane or Louise or any of the other female paramedics but, of course, since it was Anna, it felt very different.

She was a mess. Her hair was damp at the temples and there was a large wet patch all across the front of her shirt, showing him that pale blue bra he'd been interested in all day. The shirt had got twisted and untucked at the waist, too, so that a smooth triangular shape of pale skin showed at her side. With his arms around her, Finn felt it, warm and silky against his fingers.

He had an urge he'd never experienced with a woman before—to *tidy* her. He gave in to it without question, supporting her back with one hand while he brushed the damp strands of hair away from her face with the other. She held herself very still, but didn't protest.

Next, he dropped his hands to her waist and straightened the shirt. No point in trying to tuck it into that snug waistband, so he pulled it all the way out and smoothed its tail back over her hips, loving the taut, rounded feel of her shape there. Again, during the few seconds it took, she said nothing.

'You should be proud of yourself,' he told her finally.

'I am. But relieved, I suppose, more than anything. Hadn't dared to hope earlier, after this morning, that there could be a good end to the day.'

'I know,' he said softly. 'Neither had I.'

The kiss was a mistake.

It shouldn't have been, damn it, but it was. As he bent towards her mouth, he saw the alarm in her eyes, replacing the glow of what she'd called 'relief', which he knew was really a very well-deserved sense of triumph and accomplishment.

Given what Anna deserved to feel at this moment, and what he and she had both felt with each other so recently, Finn didn't want to recognise anything remotely like alarm. It made him angry, and he compounded the initial mistake of the kiss by making it deeper, more commanding and imperious and ruthless and unstoppable.

Far more than he had intended. Oh, yes. He'd meant just to paint his touch on her lips, taste her quickly. Instead, he found himself ravishing her mouth, compelling her response and stealing the warm flavour of her scent.

She responded with a tightly coiled intensity that told him there was a battle going on inside her. It angered him further. This whole thing angered him. The fact that he didn't have the control to leave her alone when she'd essentially asked him to. The fact that she wouldn't explain.

Couldn't he have it easy for once in his life? He'd really thought he'd found something here. In Anna. *With* Anna.

But apparently not. She was pulling away, her face flushed, her grey eyes blazing, and she looked as if she was about to yell at him. Or cry.

He got in first, too quickly to be in full control of what he said. 'Don't pretend you didn't enjoy that.'

'All right. I won't.'

And at that moment a nurse came out from the main desk to ask if they needed anything, the subtext being, Why are you still here?

Because I was kissing her, that's why we're still here.

'Bit of analysis,' he explained to the well-padded, frowning woman. 'We're off now, though. This superwoman just delivered a breech baby in the back of a moving ambulance.'

He squeezed Anna's shoulders automatically, then dropped his arm again as he felt her stiffen, and they hardly spoke on their way back to headquarters. Exhausted, both of them, after a day which had pulled them emotionally one way and then the other so dramatically. But there was far more to their silence than that, of course, and they both knew it.

I was so sure that we had something, he thought in frustration and more pain than he'd felt since he could remember. I really did. And now, somehow, it's all messed up and I'll be damned if it's my fault. I hate this.

CHAPTER NINE

'DON'T say it, Anna,' Kendra threatened the moment she stepped off the bus, at six-thirty on Tuesday evening.

'Say what?'

'That I look awful.'

'You look pregnant, that's all,' Anna soothed, aware that she was being more tactful than truthful.

She had seen a lot of pregnant women who looked better, including Jill Haley at the height of her labour! Jill had dropped into ambulance headquarters this morning with new baby Daniel, a bottle of wine for Finn and a big bunch of flowers for Anna. Pat, at Reception, had phoned Anna at home as it was her day off.

She had driven straight in to see the baby and collect her flowers, and was thrilled about the happy outcome of the dramatic birth for the Haley family. Little Daniel was just gorgeous, sleepy and pink, with a fuzz of golden hair, and entirely unaffected by his less than orthodox entry into the world.

Finn had been off work today, too, and she hadn't seen him.

'Yeah, a pregnant walrus,' Kendra was saying. She groaned and rubbed her back as she waddled to the side of the bus to collect her dilapidated backpack.

'Not twins, is it?' Anna teased, then wished she hadn't. Finn's twins. And twins ran in his family.

'I've asked the doctor that,' Kendra said. 'But he reckons not.'

'How was your appointment on Friday?'

'Oh, I didn't go in the end. Rob and Linda showed up early and we got talking and I completely forgot.'

'Kendra, you really shouldn't miss them!'

'I know.' She shrugged. 'Except, I mean, every time it's the same thing. Dr Little measures my stomach, he listens to the heartbeat, he weighs me, he asks the same questions.'

'Still…'

'I have another one in two weeks. He's always running late. He was probably glad I didn't show.'

Anna collected Kendra's backpack for her and carried it to the car, then they drove to her flat through the mellow light of the late summer day. She had a casserole and salad waiting, with strawberries and ice cream for dessert, and she was determined to spoil her cousin like an invalid who needed fattening up. No matter how much weight they had already gained, pregnant women needed their nourishment at a point when the baby was growing so rapidly.

They needed their rest, too. Kendra looked tired, and her hands and feet were swollen.

'It's only from the bus ride,' she said. 'Six hours of fluid draining into my ankles and fingers. The heat doesn't help either.'

'Did you get up and move around the bus?'

'Too tired, and too scared I'd fall over if we hit a bend. I'm so clumsy! And I warn you, I'll be in bed by nine. I overdid it on the weekend.'

'You'll have to let me pamper you,' Anna soothed once more.

'No arguments there!' Kendra agreed. 'Thanks so much for all this, Anna. I really appreciate it. You've no idea.'

Anna didn't mention what else she had in mind for

Kendra's open-ended visit. A meeting—or possibly con-frontation—with Finn. She had to struggle to avoid the subject tonight, but forced herself to do so, knowing that Kendra was far too tired. Too absorbed in her own dis-comfort as well, which was understandable.

Kendra wolfed down the meal, took some medicine for indigestion, had a shower and was in bed, as she had threatened to be, by nine o'clock. This left Anna with a sense of anticlimax which she knew was both unfair and illogical. Had she really expected that things might mag-ically fall into place the moment Kendra arrived in Teymouth?

Anna was back at work the next morning, and left Kendra to a lazy day, with food and cool drinks in the fridge and a lounging chair in Judy's back garden for a bit of sun-soaking if desired. Finn wasn't rostered on today, and she didn't know whether to be glad or sorry about that.

'He asked if you'd got wine from the Haleys as well, and I told him about the flowers,' Pat reported.

Finn himself phoned that night, just after she arrived home, to say, 'If you think it's sexist, we can swap.'

Growing hot at once at the sound of his voice, Anna didn't understand at first, and he apologised. 'Sorry, is my humour too obscure? I meant the wine and the flow-ers from the Haleys. I've come up with a plan for a fair split of the goodies. I'll come round with the wine and some take-aways, and you can set the table like a five-star restaurant, with the flowers in the middle.'

The suggestion at once plunged Anna into the realis-ation that she could deal with the problem between her-self, Kendra and Finn *tonight*, if she had the courage. Unknowingly, he was handing it to her on a plate. All she had to do was say yes to his half-teasing plan, but it seemed too unfair to both Kendra and Finn to spring it on them unawares.

Hearing his upbeat tone on the phone, Anna knew that for once he wasn't being fully honest about how he felt. He was trying to go ahead as if everything was all right between them, but they both knew it wasn't.

Over the past two weeks, she truly hadn't known whether to try and plan any of this or not. In the end, she had shied away from planning as being too calculating and cold-blooded, but now it seemed that improvisation might turn out to be even worse.

'I—I can't tonight,' she stammered. 'I've...got someone here. Can we make it tomorrow?'

'When those flowers will be past their best? You really want to keep them to yourself, don't you?'

'It's not the flowers.'

'Damn it, Anna, I *know* it's not the flowers!' he exploded. 'Do you think I care one iota about the flowers? But is it really that you're giving me the brush off? Don't you think a man's capable of feeling—?' He broke off. 'Look, if you want to end it, then end it, OK? I can deal with that.'

'I don't want to end it,' she said desperately, through clenched teeth.

Kendra had just walked into the living room after a late nap. She had a red mark across her blotchy face from a crease in the pillow, and she looked heavy, groggy and listless. She was massaging her temples with one hand.

'I told you, I...have something on tonight,' Anna said. 'Let's make it tomorrow.'

By which time she'd better have thought of a way of preparing both Kendra and Finn for the emotional scene that lay ahead of them.

'Tomorrow,' Finn echoed heavily. 'Sure. A'right. See you then.'

And he had put down the phone before she could say anything to soften the awkward exchange.

'Do you have any painkillers, Anna?' Kendra asked. 'I have a truly revolting headache.'

'Yes, in the bathroom cabinet,' Anna answered absently, still stewing over Finn.

Kendra disappeared for a minute, and Anna heard the mirror door of the cabinet sliding open, the rattle and pop of tablets being squeezed from a blister pack and the sound of the tap running. Kendra reappeared, looking a tiny bit better, in anticipation of the painkillers having their effect soon.

'Sounded interesting just now,' she commented.

She was obviously talking about Anna's end of the phone conversation, which was fair enough, since it wouldn't have been remotely convincing for her to pretend that she hadn't heard.

'Yes, look, it's something we badly need to talk about, actually,' Anna said. 'But first let's scramble some eggs, or something, and…and…I want to hear about *you*. Come into the kitchen while I cook, and tell me. Have you…made any decisions about the future, Kendra? After the baby's born,' she added unnecessarily.

Kendra laughed. 'The future? What's that? Can't think beyond the edge of my own stomach at the moment.'

'But you *have* to! You can't live like this, and when it affects other people…'

'Who does it affect? It's my life.'

'Finn, Kendra! It affects Finn. And anyone else who might be important in *his* life. I know it's hard for you to look beyond what's happening to your body, and beyond the birth. That's scary, giving birth for the first time. I've heard people say it's the Great Divide. B.C. and A.C., some people call it. Before Children, and After Children. But you *need* to!'

'Why, what's happening to him? Has he said something to you?'

'How could he, when he doesn't even know about the baby?'

'I mean, about someone else. Is he involved with someone else?'

'I don't know,' Anna answered, and this was closer to the truth than she wanted it to be. 'But that's why you need to tell him now, while you're here in Teymouth. Give him the chance to make things right between you. Or just to work something out. If you want me to smooth the way for you, I can invite him round here so the two of you can talk. Or take you over to his place. Tell him at work that you're in town and you'd like to see him. I want to *help* with this, Kendra!'

Kendra listened in silence to all this, then insisted stubbornly, 'It's not as simple as that.'

Anna gave up, her frustration and turmoil bringing her so close to tears that she could practically taste the salt. In the face of Kendra's attitude she had only two choices left. She could tell Finn about the baby, or she could tell Kendra, 'I'm in love with the father of your child.'

Both possibilities held all the appeal of having a tooth pulled without anaesthesia.

Ten minutes later, just as two plates of cheesy scrambled eggs on toast sat steaming on the kitchen table, the problem was taken out of her hands.

Finn arrived.

As the evening was still warm, Anna had left the outer screen door closed and the inner wooden door open, and he scarcely waited for an answer to his rattling knock on the screen door's metal frame.

Kendra was slumped at the kitchen table, looking at her nourishing dinner with a jaundiced eye, and Finn didn't see her at first. He came straight up to Anna. Didn't touch her, but obviously wanted to. Seize her by the shoulders, perhaps? His hands opened, then clenched, then opened again.

'I'm not satisfied, Anna,' he began, then stopped abruptly as Kendra rose unsteadily from the table and he caught sight of her for the first time.

'Finn!' she said in a wobbly voice. 'Uh… Hi! Lord, I feel wretched,' she added, and Anna, feeling that way herself, in spades, didn't question the statement.

'Hello, Kendra. Good to see you again.' One sweep of Finn's dark eyes took in the fact of her advanced pregnancy, but he didn't comment, and any self-consciousness that Kendra felt was overtaken by the more urgent concern of her physical state.

'Look, Anna, I feel awful,' she said. 'My headache's getting worse, and I'm seeing double. There's two of you, Finn, and one of them's *not* Craig!' She gave a dry giggle. 'That's not right, is it?'

Finn and Anna looked at each other. Anna was hot all over. Whatever she might have expected in the way of emotions filling the room, it wasn't happening, because Kendra was clearly ill, and dealing with that was the only thing that mattered right now.

'Toxaemia, it sounds like,' Finn said, and Anna nodded.

'You've been swollen in your hands and feet, haven't you, Kendra? You put it down to the bus ride and the heat, and I accepted that. I shouldn't have. Call the dispatcher, Finn?'

'Let's take her ourselves,' he said decisively. 'We know what to do if…'

She starts convulsing.

He didn't say it, but Anna understood.

'Hospital?' Kendra came in.

'You need to, Kendra,' Anna told her gently. 'This could be serious.'

Was already serious, actually, if Kendra had reached the point of having double vision.

'We'll take my car,' Finn decided. 'I brought the Holden.'

'Yes, more room in the back,' Anna agreed. 'Kendra, we're going to have you lying down in the back, OK?'

She grabbed the quilt from the bed and a couple of pillows, and Finn helped Kendra out of the flat. His car was parked in Judy's driveway, unlocked, and Anna quickly arranged the quilt and pillows in the rear seat so that Kendra could lie on her left side with her feet elevated. This should be of some help in maintaining a good blood supply to the baby and to the dangerously overloaded kidneys as well.

I should have realised, Anna was telling herself remorsefully. I should have at least done what the doctor would have done and taken her blood pressure. It must be sky-high by now. That would have told me something was wrong, but I've been so preoccupied with the issue of the baby, and Kendra telling Finn, and…

Finn was looking grim now. His mouth was set in a hard line and his eyes blazed with cold fire. It could have been just his concern over Kendra's physical condition, but Anna knew it wasn't.

No, of course it wasn't. That steely expression belonged to a man who had just realised he would imminently become a father, although the mother-to-be hadn't cared to inform him of the fact.

When Kendra was as comfortable as they could make her, Anna climbed into the front passenger seat and Finn reversed rapidly out of the driveway. He drove within the law but made better time to the hospital than an untrained driver would have done. His knuckles were tight on the wheel, and he didn't look sideways at Anna once.

In the back seat, Kendra was clearly feeling too ill to speak, and lay with her eyes closed and a hand cupped over her mouth. Anna encouraged her once or twice with updates on how close they were to the hospital, but didn't want to disturb her with any questions that required a reply.

This gave her time to feel every nuance of Finn's mood, emanating very clearly from the seat beside her. 'I know this must be a bolt from the blue, Finn,' she ventured.

'You're not wrong! You've known about this, presumably.'

'Since just before Christmas.'

'All along, in other words. From the beginning.'

'Yes. But what I didn't realise at first was—'

'Don't,' he cut in. 'It's too crazy. I don't want to hear it, a'right?'

'All right,' she agreed in a strained tone, very aware of poor Kendra in the back.

Lord, Anna had known a confrontation was brewing, and she had tried to bring it about in the best way she could, but fate was well and truly mocking her efforts now. To have it happen like this, when none of them were able to follow through.

Finn certainly didn't look pleased. Kendra didn't look

as if anything mattered at all, and Anna herself felt as if the whole thing, from day one—whenever *that* had been—was her fault.

Finn seemed to think so, too. He hadn't looked at her once. Not once. Did he think *she* should have told him?

They reached the hospital, and he pulled into the ambulance bay automatically, then swore and jerked the car forward several metres, in three erratic lurches. He swore again, and Kendra moaned. An ambulance was keening just behind them, and he couldn't block the bay.

Anna raced inside for a wheelchair and a nurse, gabbled her certainty that Kendra was in severe danger of suffering an eclamptic seizure, and led the way back to Finn's car, where he was helping Kendra to sit up and swivel her legs out to the ground. Clearly, the tablets she had taken had done nothing for her head, and she was clutching her swollen abdomen now as well.

Behind them, Anna saw Diane and Ron taking out a patient on a stretcher. They acknowledged each other briefly, and Diane pulled a face that said, What's happening?

But Anna didn't want to go into any sort of an explanation now.

'We'll admit her upstairs straight away,' said a doctor a few minutes later, after he had examined Kendra on a trolley and confirmed what Anna and Finn both knew. High blood pressure, severe swelling of hands and feet, protein in the urine and unusually brisk tendon reflexes.

'Which one of you is staying?' the doctor added. His intelligent face betrayed his uncertainty on the issue of the exact relationship between the three of them. The awkwardness in the atmosphere was palpable, even to an outsider.

'Anna?' Finn asked, his voice dry and hard. 'Since you're cousins.'

'No, *you* should,' she insisted.

'Both of you?' Dr Peter Sharpe queried hopefully.

Finn gave a brief bark of laughter, and muttered something that no one understood.

'Kendra?' Anna said gently, touching her shoulder.

'By myself,' Kendra croaked.

But that wasn't on.

'You're so stubborn, aren't you?' Anna whispered.

'Have to be.' She lapsed into silence.

'Well, for now she's coming upstairs,' Dr Sharpe said, visibly impatient now. 'The two of you work it out.'

'What's going to happen?' Anna blurted. 'Kendra needs to know.'

He frowned once more. 'Of course. I was getting to that. Kendra, we're going to monitor your condition, try and bring your symptoms under control. If we can't, you may need a Caesarean delivery. In fact, I have to say it's highly likely your baby will be born tonight. He or she will be premature, but we have the facilities here to take care of babies born at thirty-four weeks gestation and up, so you and your baby are both in very safe hands.'

Kendra managed a faint reply, and was wheeled towards the large lift. Finn and Anna were both left staring helplessly, the issue of who should go with her still unresolved. Kendra herself had said that she wanted to be alone, but—

'I'll stay, then,' Anna said coldly.

Finn simply shrugged as if indifferent to the entire issue, and Anna was so angry she would have exploded at him in any other circumstances.

Was this really what she had wanted? To find that

Finn felt so free of any connection to Kendra and the baby that he didn't even want to be present at the birth? Couldn't even manage to stay and hold Kendra's hand?

No, it wasn't what she'd wanted. It hurt. She had believed completely in Finn's decency. Those qualities of honesty and kindness had seemed apparent to her from so early on. She'd loved him for those things. Where were they now? And where did that leave the way she felt?

In a horrible, empty hole!

'This is unbelievable!' he muttered.

'Isn't it, though?' she agreed tightly.

'I'm going to go home and make some phone calls.'

'You do that.'

'Tell Kendra...'

'Yes?'

'That I'm thinking of her. Praying for her. And the baby.'

Well, at least he'd said it.

'All right.' She nodded, then she couldn't bear it any longer and turned from him to go to the lift and follow Kendra upstairs to the maternity unit on the fourth floor.

Kendra was having her observations taken and going through her medical history when Anna reached her. She already had an IV line hooked up, the fluid containing a drug which, it was hoped, would lower her blood pressure.

But obstetrician Patricia Keyes soon decided that Kendra's symptoms weren't responding to treatment and that it was dangerous for both mother and baby to wait any longer. Kendra made no protest about the imminent reality of a Caesarean delivery.

'Whatever it takes,' she said. 'What's best and safest for the baby.'

She seemed very subdued and sober, as if only now that there was a problem was she able to understand the reality of her impending motherhood.

After this, everything happened very fast. Anna was able to accompany her cousin as far as the operating theatre, but was then asked to wait outside in a small room containing a television that she didn't feel like watching and an anxious father-to-be whose wife was also undergoing an emergency Caesarean.

He looked exhausted as his wife's labour had been long and frustrating, and he'd supported her through it for nearly thirty hours before the baby's health required more dramatic action. He was summoned to meet his happy wife and new daughter while Anna was still waiting, so then she had the place to herself.

She felt ill with tension. Kendra's safety, the baby's condition, Finn's attitude. She had been so afraid of losing him to Kendra when he found out about the baby, but his apparent indifference...hostility, even...was almost worse.

She was summoned after half an hour of waiting, and the news from Dr Keyes was mixed.

'Your cousin is going to be fine. She's in Recovery now, and emerging from the anaesthesia just as she should. We'll monitor her with extra care, as problems can show up in the first twenty-four hours post-partum, but her symptoms have already subsided.'

'That's great—and the baby—?'

'She has a baby boy, and he's giving us a little more cause for concern, I'm afraid.'

'Oh, no!'

'He's smaller than we would have liked, and he has a heart murmur. We don't know how significant that's going to be at this stage, but it may need treatment in a more specialised unit.'

'Melbourne Children's?'

'You know it?'

'I'm a flight paramedic with the TAS,' Anna explained. 'I've transferred babies and children there from all over Tasmania.'

'Then you'll know he'll be in good hands if that eventuates.'

'I may even be the one who flies him there!'

'It's good that you have some experience in this area. It will help your cousin, I'm sure, to feel confident about her baby's treatment. That's great. One thing we're hoping you can clarify for us is the next of kin. The baby's father. Is he in the picture?'

'I don't know,' Anna had to say. 'I...assumed he would be, but that's in doubt now. It might take a while until they work things out.'

The obstetrician nodded. She had encountered situations like this before. So had Anna. It didn't help on this occasion. She swallowed what she felt and asked if she could see Kendra and the baby.

'Of course. Try and reassure her if you can. The baby's long-term outlook is good, but it may not be an easy road.'

Kendra was very groggy after the general anaesthesia, and in pain from the surgery, despite medication.

'When will they let me see him?' she wanted to know, her voice fuzzy.

'They'll take you down to the premmie unit in an hour or two,' Anna said, squeezing Kendra's hand.

'What's he like? Have you seen him?'

'Not yet. I will in a minute, but I'll just have to peer

through the window, I expect. I'll come and tell you about him, shall I?'

'Yes, please. I can't... I mean, he doesn't feel real yet. But I miss him. It's weird. I don't like it. I want him.'

'Do you have a name for him?'

Kendra hesitated. 'After our grandfather, I thought, Anna.'

'Stephen.' She nodded. 'Your mum will like that.' So would Anna's.

Anna wanted to mention Finn, but knew that the subject was too emotional for both of them.

After ten minutes she went to look at baby Stephen, who was frighteningly small but safely under the watchful care of a fully trained nurse in the special care baby unit. He had silky black hair all over his head, a red face, no eyebrows and a further fuzz of downy dark hair over his shoulders and back, which would soon wear away. Somehow he didn't quite look finished. 'Not quite cooked yet,' some of the special care nurses would say of their tiny charges.

And yet, somehow, what she told Kendra when she returned to the recovery ward was absolutely true.

'He's beautiful!'

It was ten-thirty.

It felt as if it should have been much later but, in fact, everything had happened very fast. As she left the hospital, Anna found herself wishing it was two in the morning, then she might have had an excuse for *not* doing what she knew she had to do.

She took a taxi home, paid the driver, then went inside to freshen up a little and dry her parched throat with a drink of cold water. On the kitchen table sat the two plates of cold, congealed scrambled eggs on toast. Anna surveyed them without appetite of any kind and left them alone.

Then she went out to her car and drove to Finn's. The lights were still on, and as she walked past the kitchen window she could see him standing at the sink, rinsing out a plate and a mug.

He must have seen her shadow crossing the rectangle of light thrown by the window because he looked up as she passed and met her at the front door before she'd had time to knock.

'You have a son, Finn,' she told him at once.

'Do I?' There was a black edge to his voice.

'Named Stephen. After Kendra's and my grandfather. I thought you'd like to know.'

'Doing well?' He was leaning one hand heavily on the doorknob, making the open door move and creak a little.

'Better than he could be,' she said. 'Not as well as the doctors want. He's small, and they're talking about a heart defect. He may have to go to Melbourne.'

'That's convenient.'

She took it as sarcasm, and agreed in biting tones, 'Yes, out of sight, out of mind, as far as you're concerned.'

He laughed jerkily as if it hurt his stomach—the way Kendra would be laughing for the next few days. He obviously didn't plan to invite her in, which was good because she wouldn't have gone. She wondered why she had thought it necessary to come in person, instead of delivering a terse report by phone.

'Well, that's all,' she said, falsely bright. 'Sleep well, Finn.'

'I won't.'

'No, neither will I.'

Tear-blinded, she went back to the car and sat at the wheel for several minutes before she was able to start the engine.

Listening to her drive away, aware to the minute of how long she had sat out there in the car, Finn tried to pull apart the strands of feeling inside him, tangled like barbed wire. He discovered anger and pain and a love that he really didn't want to feel at the moment, but felt anyway.

There were questions he couldn't answer. Where did his sense of betrayal come from? And why hadn't he told her the truth? Was he punishing her? Or himself? Or was this really the end between them, and therefore the truth didn't matter?

If she didn't hear it from him, she'd hear it from someone eventually. Sooner rather than later probably. He wondered how she would react then.

He also wondered how he would manage to work with her tomorrow. He thought about trying to change his roster, get himself partnered with someone else, then decided it would be too obvious. If no one at headquarters had yet guessed for certain that he was in love with Anna Brewster, he certainly didn't want them to suspect that their fragile young relationship had failed. They were both professionals. They'd just have to get through it.

And they did, of course. No dramas the next day. An elderly woman with dizzy spells. An even older and very terminal cancer patient to take to the hospice. A child with painful but moderate and easily treatable burns.

Finn and Anna both held themselves together very well, talking politely to each other when necessary, ignoring each other when not, using their patients as chap-

erons, safeguarding themselves against the blurting of
ill-chosen words.

Until the very end of the day, when they were both
preparing to go home and Finn couldn't stand his feelings or Anna's tight, hunted face a moment longer.

She was standing in the little storage room just off the
vehicle bay, the place where they had both stood that
first day, bristling at each other over coffee. She looked
like an animal seeking refuge until she saw him, and
then she looked like a cornered fox.

But she lifted her chin and brazened it out. 'Are you
off now, Finn?'

'Yes. I'll see you tomorrow.'

'Uh-huh.'

Look at the spurt of colour in her cheeks! Look at the
way her grey eyes glittered! He wanted to take her in
his arms and…shake her? Yell at her?

No! *Kiss* her! Tell her how angry he was at her mis-
judgement of him, and at her willingness over the past
few weeks to blunder forward in her relationship with
him, believing what she did.

And then, once again, when he was done with angry
words, kiss her senseless and silly and insist that none
of it mattered. But she looked so simmeringly, *volcani-
cally* furious at him—which she had *absolutely* no right
to be—that all he could do was spit out the simple and
to him blindingly obvious truth.

CHAPTER TEN

WATCHING Finn in the doorway, Anna berated herself silently. What on earth do I want from him? Why does my body have to betray me like this?

The strength had drained from her legs at the sudden sight of him, like ice cream melting in a hot frying-pan, and it made about as much sense as this illogical comparison, too.

He looked as tense and tightly wound as she felt, and yet the smouldering fire of his anger suited him somehow. It emphasised the power in his shoulders, the intelligence in his eyes, the strength of his capacity to feel. Looking at him, she had a sudden image, which she at once tried to block out, of the way his face and body would look in the throes of heartfelt love-making.

And then, while she was still battling with her imagination, he spoke once more, a casual, almost throwaway line that stayed hanging in the air after he disappeared from the doorway, and was punctuated by the rhythm of his departing footsteps.

'By the way, Anna, that baby isn't mine.'

She was too shocked to react or even take it in at first. Not his? But Kendra had said—

What *had* she said, exactly? Anna couldn't remember any of her cousin's actual words, but she knew she wasn't wrong in her certainty that Kendra had intended to claim Finn as her baby's father.

None of it made sense.

In a daze, she went home to change and force down

something to eat. She'd had no appetite for breakfast this morning, and hardly any for lunch, and even though she still didn't actually feel hungry, she knew she couldn't go on giving in to the squeamishness of her churning stomach.

Then she drove to the hospital, wondering how she could possibly confront her cousin less than twenty-four hours after an emergency Caesarean which had only by a narrow squeak saved Kendra's life and her child's.

In the end, however, the question was moot. There, in Kendra's room in the maternity unit, on an upright padded chair beside her bed, sat Finn.

No. *Not* Finn.

A rougher, more awkward-looking and to Anna's eyes infinitely less dear version of Finn—his twin brother Craig. They weren't identical, but the resemblance was very strong.

Embarrassed, Kendra introduced them, then sent Craig away to the special care baby unit to look at what was now unquestionably *his* son.

'Tell me what's going on, Kendra,' Anna said.

'I don't know yet,' Kendra confessed. 'I was amazed to see him. I honestly didn't think he'd want to know.'

'Finn told him?' It was the only thing that made sense.

'Phoned him last night,' Kendra confirmed.

'Then Finn's not—' Anna broke off and started again. 'All this time, when I've been trying to persuade you to talk to him...'

Again, the enormity of it robbed her of words.

Kendra shifted uncomfortably. 'Don't yell at me, Anna,' she said. 'You see, it was just a one-night stand with Craig. I—I wanted Finn. I thought he was interested at first. I...guess I tried to seduce him at that party I told you about, but he sort of turned me down. He was too much of a gentleman about it, that was the trouble.'

'Too much of a...?'

'Too nice about it. You know. Courteous regret, sort of thing. Made me feel like I could get him if I kept trying. If I played my cards right, you know what I mean? Only I stupidly took the consolation prize on offer that night, the one who was up for it.'

'Craig.' Anna nodded, masking her discomfort at Kendra's rather crude terminology.

'We'd both been drinking,' Kendra went on. 'Craig and I,' she clarified, unnecessarily. 'Shouldn't have happened, but it did, and then there I was, pregnant, still wanting Finn. *Thinking* I wanted him, I guess.'

She shrugged.

'And Craig had another relationship he was ending at the time,' she went on. 'He wasn't in the right place to deal with my news, so I didn't tell him. The whole thing was hopeless and, as I said, I didn't have any money or a job, so I just left Melbourne and went back home. I *wanted* my baby to be Finn's. Oh, I did! But I knew being pregnant wasn't the best time to try and hook a man. I thought maybe when I had my figure back, and my skin, and this cute little baby.'

'So you and Craig...'

Kendra shrugged once more. 'He's pretty shocked. About being a father. He wants to be involved in some way, but we're not sure how yet.'

'Kendra...'

'I know.' She closed her eyes. 'You don't have to give a point by point analysis of how I've stuffed up my life.'

'I wasn't going to.'

'You've always been the one who knew where you were going, and made the right decisions and choices.'

'That's not true.'

'Anyway…' Kendra sat up straighter, and there was a new look on her face, more determined and clear-eyed than anything Anna had seen there before. 'You wouldn't believe what I feel about Stephen,' she said. 'Honestly, Anna. I don't know what it means yet. All I know is that for the first time in my life I have a guiding star. His well-being. Hell!' She blinked back tears. 'His *survival,* at the moment. And I'll do whatever it takes.'

She would have said more, Anna knew, but at that moment Craig appeared in the doorway once more, looking gob-smacked and happy at the same time. He plunked himself back down in the chair beside the bed and took Kendra's hand in a tight squeeze between both of his, as if he hardly knew he was doing it.

'He's…he's incredible,' he stammered. 'Brave. A fighter, Kendra, I can see that a'ready.' It was startling to hear Finn's accent emerging from another man's mouth. 'Looks like me,' he went on. 'And you. Your mouth, I think. When will they know? About his heart, I mean.'

'They're monitoring it,' Kendra said. 'They don't want to do anything invasive, you see, so they just have to wait and see how it develops. They might have to send him to Melbourne.'

'Will you go, too?'

Kendra laughed. 'Try suggesting anything else!'

'There's a spare room at my place. You're welcome to stay there.'

'Thanks, Craig.' She returned the pressure of his hand and a smile crept into her face.

'You did really well, Kendra.'

She nodded and then shook her head. 'No, *he* did

really well. He survived, and he's strong and they're going to let me try and feed him soon.'

'Can I stay?' Craig asked.

'If you'd like to.'

They smiled at each other again. Tentatively. Like the sun trying to come out at the end of a dull day.

Anna had to clear her throat before she could say, 'I'm going to head off, Kendra, OK?'

'OK, Anna.'

'Are you staying with Finn, Craig?' Anna asked.

He looked vague. 'I suppose so. Still have my overnight bag here under the bed. I came straight from the airport. I have his address. Might not make it out there till pretty late. Will you be seeing him, or something?'

'Uh, no, I shouldn't think so.'

'Right.' He nodded, not particularly interested.

So she left. Just went home and forced down another meal she didn't want, and waited for something to happen. Some miracle that would ease this aching, queasy feeling in her stomach. But nothing did, and she went to bed that night and got up the next morning with the knowledge that she and Finn had another day of crewing together to get through, while trying to pretend to a whole host of colleagues, patients and their relatives that nothing was wrong.

She wished they had been on a flight crew today, because at least the noise of the aircraft and the necessity for headphones would have masked painful silences somewhat.

Encountering Finn at headquarters, she could see at once that he hadn't softened his attitude, and this fact rekindled her own anger so that it throbbed inside her as painfully as her hurt.

Why was he punishing her like this? Was it her fault

that Kendra had deceived her, as a side-effect to Kendra's own self-deception? Surely it wasn't!

But Finn didn't seem to agree.

They avoided each other around the ambulance station, diligently chatting with other colleagues or catching up on busy work that really didn't need to be done. Car 119 was the cleanest, shiniest and best-equipped vehicle in the fleet today, thanks to a solid hour of meticulous attention from Anna.

They didn't get called out until two, but then the momentum of the day changed quickly, as it was a priority one call-out, in response to the trembling voice of an elderly woman whose husband had had a 'funny turn' in front of his favourite daytime television show, and couldn't get up from the couch.

It was a stroke. They discovered this on arriving at an attractive suburban house, where flowers were a feature both in the lovingly cared-for gardens and the cosy living room.

Mrs Abbott was crying when she met them at the door. 'He's breathing. But he still hasn't moved and his face looks so still. Like stone. He's trying to talk, but he can't.'

Definitely a stroke of some kind. Seventy-eight-year-old Stanley Abbott betrayed several classic symptoms. He was unable to move or speak clearly, and one side of his face was slack. It was too early to predict how he'd fare in the long term, but Mrs Abbott clearly feared the worst.

'If only he'd speak to me,' she sobbed.

Beside her, their patient looked agitated, too. He was making little sounds, and lifting a shoulder inefficiently.

Anna had to calm Mrs Abbott down before she could get her to focus on practicalities, such as packing a bag

with things her husband might need and asking a neighbour to drive her to the hospital.

'People often can't speak at first,' she soothed. 'But
it's amazing how much speech they can get back later
on.'

'But we hadn't spoken to each other all day, you see,'
Eileen Abbott explained, still tearful. 'He got cross with
me because I forgot to pay the credit card bill, and I said
it didn't matter, it'd only cost us a few dollars in interest,
and he said I was always wasting money like that, and
we both got into a huff and wouldn't talk, and now he
might never talk to me again.'

'Of course he will!' Anna said urgently. 'He'll talk to
you right now.'

She could see that Mrs Abbott was becoming more
agitated, not less, and that every bit of what she felt was
reflected in her husband's stroke slackened features. She
pulled Mrs Abbott over to sit next to her husband, who
would be transferred to a stretcher in a moment, then
propped him up and got both of them to hold hands.

'It's all right, isn't it, Mr Abbott?' she said to him
very clearly. 'You're not cross with Eileen any more,
are you? It was just a little, little thing, and you both
blew up, but it's over now and it doesn't matter. Do you
want to give her a kiss?'

Another little sound. Anna chose to assume it meant
yes. It *looked* as if it meant yes, and Mrs Abbott leaned
forward while Mr Abbott managed to press his face to
her cheek.

'Uv,' he said very clearly, then again, '*Uv!*' And there
were tears in his eyes.

His wife understood. 'I love you, too, Stan,' she said.
'I really do! Now, let's calm down and get ourselves
organised, shall we?'

She was on her feet seconds later, untying her apron and bustling about, and both of them looked markedly more at ease.

It was possible…probable…that their marriage had entered a challenging new phase today, but the fact that it had been marked by an open statement of love on both sides was good and important.

Finn and Anna left Mrs Abbott with the companionship of her neighbour, an older woman like herself. Mrs Abbott planned to ring her son and daughter, pack some toiletries and other things for her husband and then follow on to the hospital. In the ambulance, Anna drove and Finn sat with Stan Abbott in the back.

'Some movement returning in your right arm now, Mr Abbott,' Anna heard him say as they reached the hospital. 'You couldn't do that before, could you? When we were getting you onto the stretcher? That's a very good sign.'

Half an hour later, they were back in the big vehicle bay at headquarters after another silent journey. Anna went to jump out of the vehicle in the brisk manner she was hiding behind today, but Finn stopped her with a hand on her arm.

'Don't go in yet,' he said. 'I've got something to say to you, Anna.'

'Yes?' She knew her face had tightened. Couldn't help it. She folded her arms across her front, knowing what a defensive gesture it was but needing it so that her body didn't betray how much it…*she*…needed him.

His eyes were glittering darkly, and there was a brooding energy to him that she still didn't trust. Was this going to be an attack? Or…?

'I guess Mr Abbott summed it up really,' he said.

'Mr Abbott didn't say very much,' Anna answered crisply.

'No, but what he did say…'

'All he said was "Uv".'

'Exactly. And if I could get away with it, that's all I'd say, too, only we've got ourselves into too much of a mess for that, haven't we, Anna?'

'Wouldn't disagree with that,' she answered, still thinking about the 'uv' bit.

'Hell, *how* could you think that baby was mine?' he burst out at last, and the words galvanised her.

'How?' she stormed back: 'Because Kendra as good as told me he was. Barely mentioned Craig. *Only* talked about you, and about protecting *you*, being fair to *you*. What else was I to think, when she was deceiving herself even more than she was deceiving me? Why are you so angry?'

'Not angry,' he growled. 'Disgusted. At myself. For loving a woman who'd go after a man—'

'Did I "go after" you?'

'No. Course you didn't.'

'Then use the right words.'

'Let's get out of this damned ambulance first.'

'And go where?'

'Don't care. Stand-down room with the door shut. Somewhere where I can hold you and kiss you till we're both gasping.'

'But you're disgusted with me? Gee, that makes sense!'

They got out of their respective doors and…well… slammed them, if the truth be told. The sound echoed around the vehicle bay and one or two interested faces looked in their direction.

'Disgusted?' he echoed, then sighed. 'No. It's strange.

Other times I'd just have bailed out if something like this had happened. Said goodbye and meant it. No regrets. This time I didn't even think about it. Knew I wasn't going to do that, knew I was going to have it out with you, but I didn't know when, and how, I was going to get past—'

'Sounds as if you still don't. *We* still don't.' She wasn't going to let him think it was all one-sided, because it wasn't. She was angry and frustrated, too.

He scraped his fingers briefly against her palm as they walked up the stairs towards the stand-down rooms, but the gesture of closeness didn't hold, and when they entered the grey corridor he dropped back and let her walk in front. She was aware of him behind her, the way she'd have been aware of a great thick stormcloud approaching behind her on an open highway.

Inevitably, he was going to catch up, and all hell would break loose. This wasn't over yet, she knew. If too many rash things were said, and not enough said that was right...

The stand-down room seemed very small when he closed the door on the rest of the world. She faced him, her arms folded, and invited tautly, 'Talk, Finn.'

'OK.'

He prowled. Not much room for that, so he fetched up six inches from her and stopped, and she crumpled at the knees and sat on the bed, because she wasn't ready to touch him yet.

'This is what I can't get my head around, Anna,' he said in a more controlled tone. 'That you thought Kendra was carrying my baby, but you were still ready to get involved, without saying anything to me about it.'

'But I *wasn't* ready to get involved!' she pointed out. 'I fought it, Finn. You must have felt that.'

'You didn't fight it for long.'

'OK, so either I'm weak, or what I felt was very strong. Take your pick.'

He was silent, then said, '*Was* very strong?'

'*Is* strong,' she admitted. '*Is*, Finn. Isn't that what you were saying in the car? As soon as I decided to stop fighting it, I knew I had to talk to you about Kendra and the baby. It was on the day we went to the beach together, remember? I was primed to have this big, important talk with you, but then what you said about parttime fatherhood, about not wanting that if you could possibly help it, made me realise something I'd never considered. I was working on all the wrong assumptions, I suddenly thought, because you didn't know. Didn't know about the baby at all.'

'You had thought until then that I was the kind of man who'd turn his back completely on his own child?'

'No!' she burst out in frustration. 'I was quite certain that you *weren't* that kind of a man, and that didn't make sense until I discovered you didn't know, at which point I got hit with a whole new swag of dilemmas.'

'Yeah?'

'Well, one huge dilemma, really. You *had* to know before I could freely go further with what had started to happen, and yet I couldn't be the one to tell you. Kendra had to do it. If she was having your baby, if she was hoping for some kind of shared involvement with the child, she *had* to be the one to tell you. I persuaded her to come down, but that eleven-day wait seemed agonising, and I was still trying to persuade her to talk to you when you showed up the other night and her toxaemia reached crisis point.'

'Which was when it hit me what you thought about Kendra and me,' Finn came in. 'And I was so angry with you for doubting my...my honour, I suppose, since that's one of the things I really wanted to offer you, Anna. I wanted to offer you my honour. I guess that's old-fashioned, isn't it?'

'Not to me.'

'Isn't it?'

'Not at all.'

He sat on the bed beside her, and she looked into his face, which she couldn't read. It was very serious. His brows were lowered and his mouth was tight, with his jaw rigid and square.

'Do you still want to offer me that?' she said quietly after a moment, afraid of the answer. 'I mean, you're right,' she went on before he could reply.

This was the heart of the matter. She groped for the right words, hardly aware that he'd taken her hand and was chafing it with his fingers.

'Knowing you,' she began carefully, looking down now. She added her other hand to the tangle of fingers resting on her thigh and he squeezed it. They gripped each other, as if letting go of the contact would tear them apart. 'And—and loving you,' she went on, 'I should have realised that it made no sense, that if the baby had been yours, you would have behaved very differently from the moment you saw Kendra in my kitchen. I'm sorry, Finn. If sorry is enough.'

She looked up at last, frightened of what she might read in his face, despite what he had said.

'Of course it's enough,' he said gruffly. 'Hell, do you think I'm that much of a fool?'

And his mouth brushed hers, then lingered to set them both on fire. It wasn't the most elegant kiss in the world. Too hungry for that. Too happy and scared and needful. Anna could hardly breathe. Finn had his eyes closed and his hands buried in the fabric of her shirt. When they slid upwards to claim her breasts through the smooth satin of her bra, they both shuddered, tore their mouths apart, pressed their foreheads together, then kissed again.

'I suppose what all this is really telling us,' he said slowly, some time later, 'is that we don't know each other well enough yet.' Then he grinned, and his dark eyes lit up like flame. 'Funny how that doesn't stop me from loving you, though, Anna.'

'Doesn't it?' she said. 'Doesn't it, Finn?' Her heart was beating wildly.

'In the end?' he whispered, sliding his arms around her and crushing her mouth against his once more. 'After we've been angry and yelled at each other? And explained and apologised and all the rest of it?'

'After all that,' she agreed.

'Not one…tiny…bit,' he told her, and pulled her down onto the bed.

EPILOGUE

THE baby was crying.

'The pressure change is as slight as we can make it, but it still might be hurting his ears,' Anna said into her headphones, above the noise of the aircraft. 'Let's try that dummy, Kendra.'

'OK.' Her cousin nodded, and passed it across.

The Kingair had started its descent into Melbourne. On take-off from Teymouth, little Stephen had been soothed with a bottle of Kendra's expressed breast milk, but that was all gone now, and he wouldn't yet be ready for another one.

'He's handling this well,' Finn commented.

He was monitoring the readouts on the equipment. Heartbeat, respiration rate and blood gases all fine.

At three months, Stephen was growing steadily. He'd had some ups and downs at first, and had remained in hospital where his heart defect and its symptoms could be properly treated until he was deemed ready for surgery. That milestone had now been reached, and he was on his way to Melbourne with Kendra, in Anna's and Finn's care, for his surgery.

Craig had remained in Teymouth for several days following his son's birth, but had then returned to Melbourne in order to keep his new job in landscape gardening. He had been able to return to Teymouth for weekends twice more over the past three months, staying with Finn each time, while Kendra was still living at Anna's.

Nothing had yet been said about the future of their tentative relationship, but the signs were good. Both the new parents seemed to have Stephen's welfare at the very top of their priority list, and that was a crucial start.

Stephen was still crying, too upset to take and hold the pacifying dummy in his mouth as he needed to for comfort. Kendra looked worried.

'He might take my finger instead,' she said. 'If I could wipe it first, just to make sure it's clean.'

Anna found a disposable wipe and Kendra very seriously swabbed her little finger with it, then put it in the baby's mouth, stroking it against the sensitive skin of his upper palate. This time he responded, and the strenuous sucking soon did the trick, soothing him into silence.

'Thank goodness,' Kendra said. 'Craig is supposed to be meeting us at the hospital. I bet he's nervous about the surgery. I am...'

'A couple of weeks and Stephen will be flying home again,' Anna said to encourage her cousin's positive thinking.

But Kendra shook her head and confessed self-consciously, 'I'm hoping this is going to be a one-way trip. Craig wants the three of us to find a place together and give Stephen a chance at having two parents. I...kind of have a good feeling about it, too. When he suggested it, I said yes.'

'That's wonderful, Kendra,' Anna exclaimed. 'You hadn't said anything about it until now.'

'Scared to,' Kendra admitted. 'But when we talked on the phone last night, he sounded really sure.'

They were on the ground in Melbourne for over three hours, with the journey to and from the airport to complete, as well as the transfer from plane to ambulance, and then from ambulance to paediatric unit. As promised, Craig was at the hospital already, and when he and Kendra stood together beside their baby's high-tech hospital cot, the three of them looked like a family.

Back on the plane, Finn said to Anna, 'That took a bit longer than I thought it would.'

'Usually does, to Melbourne,' she replied. 'The ground time and preparation for take-off eat up the time.'

'Hope we're not going to be late back.'

'I'm feeling positive today,' she told him softly.

'I'm not,' he growled, and leaned closer, threatening a kiss. 'And if everyone decides we're not going to show, and gives up and goes home...'

Anna rediscovered something she'd learned already when it came to Finn. When he felt something, she caught it. By the time the plane landed in Teymouth, and they'd gone through the final flight protocols, she was a bundle of impatience and nerves. They each had precisely forty minutes to get home, shower and dress for a three-o'clock wedding.

Their own.

The conflicting demands of both family and working lives had meant that this was their best opportunity, short of waiting until next spring, and they had seized on it, even though it meant that Kendra and Craig and baby Stephen wouldn't be present.

It was a simple and intimate occasion, just the way both of them wanted it, and was to be held in the park near Anna's flat. Present would be both sets of parents, Anna's brother Rod, Judy Lawton, Vern Land, some more friends from work and elsewhere. There would be a short yet romantic ceremony, conducted by a civil marriage celebrant. They'd each chosen a poem to add to the traditional vows. Finally, a late afternoon picnic meal of champagne and hot and cold savouries and petits fours was scheduled, to be finished off by a cake decorated with ivory sugar lace.

Their autumn honeymoon would be a lazy two weeks of driving in Finn's classic Holden around Tasmania, and they planned on going just where whim took them. They both wanted it that way. No flying, please. No hectic schedules. Who needed any of that? Certainly not two flight paramedics.

The past three months had unfolded like the unfurling of a perfect flower, their relationship deepening into the full intimacy of love-making and the certainty that they wanted to share their future for a whole lifetime.

Strangely, this inner certainty didn't stop the bridal nerves, Anna found.

With the minutes ticking by, no bride had ever donned a white silk slip and simply cut silk overdress with greater speed or shakier fingers, and it was fortunate that Judy Lawton had once trained as a hairdresser. She helped Anna to achieve a piled-up look with combs and pins in precisely three minutes.

And when they reached the park, Finn was waiting in front of the gathering of guests, with Vern at his side as best man. Finn had dressed with shaky fingers, too, Anna guessed. His dark grey tie was half a centimetre crooked, against the background of a steel-coloured shirt and darker suit.

Did it matter about the tie? Not a bit. Anna straightened it anyway, immediately after the ceremony. It was her first act as his bride.

'You haven't even kissed me,' Finn began in an indignant whisper as her fingers reached for the knot at his throat.

But Anna had remedied the objection before the

words were even out of his mouth. She leaned close, her hand still at his neck, and lifted her face to his. She had a moment in which to see the flare of desire and love that brightened the depths of his eyes, then he held her and found her mouth.

They stood together in the late, gentle sunlight, wrapped motionless in each other's arms for quite a bit longer than was customary. Finn's down-to-earth and gruff-voiced father had to resort to ironic applause to end the moment, and everyone laughed. For Anna's mother, the laughter came through tears.

'Never mind. There's more where that one came from,' Anna murmured to her new husband, tangling her fingers in his as they went to receive a barrage of hugs and congratulations.

Rod was beaming down from his gangly height. There were tears in Judy's eyes. Dad had his sinewy arm around Mum's comfortable waist. Finn's mother had her hands clasped together over her heart.

'Hope so...' Finn said, and tested her claim straight away by nuzzling against her ear. 'I want a whole lifetime more of this.'

By five o'clock that evening, they were happily driving west, into a golden autumn sunset, still dressed in their simple wedding clothes and covered in confetti. Finn's yellow car rattled loudly, a cacophony of joyous noise made by two dozen tin cans which Vern and Judy had conspired to attach at the back, giggling more during the process than two divorcees in their forties should have done.

At a superficial glance, they made a pair of unlikely conspirators, but Anna and Finn had their suspicions.

'You know, I have a very good feeling about those two,' Finn said as he and Anna drove away.

'Yeah?' She glanced back through the rear window and watched the pair clapping and grinning gleefully. 'You might be right.'

'Of course I'm right. I have an intuition about these things,' he said smugly.

'Men always do, of course,' she agreed, humouring him.

'They do!' he argued. 'Men are much more romantic than women, when it comes to the crunch.'

'Finn—'

'Honestly. We just don't believe in showing it.'

'Hmm.' Sliding closer to him on the bench seat and leaning her head on his confetti-covered shoulder, Anna remained sceptical, but looked forward to the possibility of being convinced.

And behind them, as the sound of their car faded into the distance, Vern was saying to Judy, with a misty sort of smile and a far-away look in his eyes, 'You know, I have a very good feeling about those two.'

Judy, who was very tired of being divorced and extremely impressed with Vern, simply smiled at him, nodded energetically and sighed.

MILLS & BOON®

Makes any time special™

Mills & Boon publish 29 new titles every month. Select from...

Modern Romance™   Tender Romance™

Sensual Romance™

Medical Romance™   Historical Romance™

MAT2

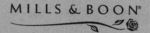

Medical Romance™

EMERGENCY REUNION *by Abigail Gordon*

The man she had loved and lost eight years before was back in Dr Hannah Morgan's life as her new boss! Now a father, Kyle Templeton was still bitter, but Hannah was beginning to wonder if all three of them had been given a second chance.

A BABY FOR JOSEY *by Rebecca Lang*

When Nurse Josey Lincoln confided in Dr Guy Lake about her desperate fear that she could never have a baby – he offered to help! But even if he could give her a baby, he couldn't give her *himself*, and she began to realise that she wanted Guy most of all...

THE VISITING CONSULTANT *by Leah Martyn*

When Josh meets nurse Alex Macleay during a medical emergency, the mutual attraction is too much to ignore. He wants a casual summer affair, but Alex wants a husband and a father for her little girl – and Josh is the ideal candidate!

On sale 3rd August 2001

Available at most branches of WH Smith, Tesco, Martins, Borders, Easons, Sainsbury, Woolworth and most good paperback bookshops

0701/03b

A Perfect Family

An enthralling family saga by bestselling author

PENNY JORDAN

Published 20th July

*Available at branches of WH Smith, Tesco,
Martins, RS McCall, Forbuoys, Borders, Easons,
Sainsbury, Woolworth and most good paperback bookshops*

4 FREE

books and a surprise gift!

We would like to take this opportunity to thank you for reading this Mills & Boon® book by offering you the chance to take FOUR more specially selected titles from the Medical Romance™ series absolutely FREE! We're also making this offer to introduce you to the benefits of the Reader Service™—

- ★ FREE home delivery
- ★ FREE gifts and competitions
- ★ FREE monthly Newsletter
- ★ Exclusive Reader Service discounts
- ★ Books available before they're in the shops

Accepting these FREE books and gift places you under no obligation to buy, you may cancel at any time, even after receiving your free shipment. Simply complete your details below and return the entire page to the address below. *You don't even need a stamp!*

YES! Please send me 4 free Medical Romance books and a surprise gift. I understand that unless you hear from me, I will receive 6 superb new titles every month for just £2.49 each, postage and packing free. I am under no obligation to purchase any books and may cancel my subscription at any time. The free books and gift will be mine to keep in any case.

M1ZEA

Ms/Mrs/Miss/Mr ....Initials.....................................
BLOCK CAPITALS PLEASE

Surname ....

Address ....

....

....Postcode...................................

Send this whole page to:
UK: FREEPOST CN81, Croydon, CR9 3WZ
EIRE: PO Box 4546, Kilcock, County Kildare (stamp required)